W

Forbidden Worlds . . .

GANYMEDE

Where men and women of Earth are imprisoned by mysterious creatures and a beautiful girl with floating hair!

THE MOON

Where an earthly sleuth combs an outland rich with uranium ore, and is shadowed by an ancient, underground race!

VENUS

Where a tyranny of Hags rules, and a band of rebels mounts a daring challenge!

Planets Three

FREDERICK POHL

PLANETS THREE

BERKLEY BOOKS, NEW YORK

PLANETS THREE

A Berkley Book / published by arrangement with
the author

PRINTING HISTORY
Berkley edition / January 1982

ISBN: 0–425–05224–9

A BERKLEY BOOK ® TM 757,375

Contents

Introduction

For the first fifteen years of my life as a professional writer, which is to say the period when I began to be paid for what I wrote (though not very much, and unfortunately not very often), I wrote under pen names. This was partly because of romantic notions about authorship—using a pseudonym was part of the glamor—but also partly out of simple prudence. Even when those earliest stories happened to get published, I knew they weren't very good. The fact that my real name was not on them gave me a chance to slide out from under the responsibility when the reactions were bad. It also gave me the option of claiming credit in the event that they were really well liked . . . but that did not often happen.

So I used at least a dozen different names, some all my own, many of them to mask collaborations with Cyril Kornbluth, Dirk Wylie and other equally new-hatched writer friends. "Elton V. Andrews" was the first pseudonym I used, and all my own. (Not that anyone would wish to dispute it with me.) "S. D. Gottesman" was usually Cyril and me, but once or twice other members of the Futurians were involved. "Paul Dennis Lavond" was meant to be a three-way by-line for Dirk, Bob Lowndes and myself—but wasn't always. "Warren F. Howard", I think, was just me, on one or two stories. But the pen name I preferred for my own work, and the name under which the following three stories were originally published, was "James Mac-Creigh." I have no idea why I picked that particular name. I do know why I picked that *kind* of name, and it was by following the advice of John W. Campbell.

Throughout those fifteen years, from 1937 to 1952, John Campbell was the mightiest editor in science fiction. In my view, he still is. He picked the science-fiction field up and shaped it between his hands before he set it down again; it has been permanently improved ever since. He did it by bringing new writers into the field, and above all by advising and counseling, not to say nagging, every science-fiction writer who would listen to him. Most did. I *always* did, even when the advice was not all that good. It was John's notion that science-fiction readers did not like "foreign" names, especially when those names were attached to stories. What sf readers wanted was good Amurrican by-lines, and what kind of by-lines were those? Why, Scotch-Irish, of course. So I mulled over that thought on the subway home from his office, and by the time I reached Brooklyn I had a new pseudonym. (It didn't help. In all his thirty-four-year tenure as editor of *Astounding/Analog*, John never published a story that was all my own, under "James MacCreigh" or any other name.)

To John's great credit, he did not usually retain his bad ideas after he found out they were bad. He gave up on the Scotch-Irish by-lines fairly early in his career, after the ice had been demonstrated to be broken by the Isaac Asimovs and Stanley G. Weinbaums who had got their start elsewhere, and were obviously too good to be fooled with.

And I gave up "James MacCreigh" too. These three

stories were about the last to be published under that name. By the time they came out, in the postwar 1940s, I had developed enough confidence and courage to risk putting my own name on what I wrote.

In the three or four years at the end of the 1930s, just before the United States got into World War II, the science-fiction field was booming.

I don't mean financially. There wasn't much money around. No magazine paid much more than a penny a word, and most paid less—a *lot* less, when you come to Don Wollheim's *Stirring* and *Cosmic*, which generally paid the authors nothing at all. But there were more than a dozen magazines, where in all of previous history there had never been more than two or three at a time.

The war blew them almost all away. Paper got expensive, then scarce, then rationed. Writers got drafted. So did editors. Some went into war work—Cyril Kornbluth went up to Connecticut to run a lathe instead of a typewriter; Isaac Asimov, L. Sprague de Camp and Robert A. Heinlein went to do research at the Philadelphia Navy Yard. Street & Smith managed to keep *Astounding* alive all through the hostilities—not easily. Most of the other science-fiction publishers just gave up. For four or five years, from about 1942 until things settled down after the war, there was not much time for writing science fiction, or much point in it. When I went into the Air Force on April Fool's Day of 1943 *Figurehead* was about half written. It stayed in mothballs until I was a civilian again; and so did a lot of other stories, by a lot of other writers.

Then came the great days of 1945. Democracy was rescued. Peace and freedom were assured forever. And we all got back to our lives.

Emerging from a major war is a lot like being born again. All the old habits and ties are canceled or weakened. Shadowy opportunities offer on every hand. I had a brand-new wife, Dorothy LesTina, acquired in Paris the year before; a brand-new apartment in Greenwich Village (where else should a writer live?); and a brand-new career in advertising, begun on April Fool's Day of 1946.

It was a confusing and promising time. I knew what I wanted to do with my life. Writing was it. I was a lot less sure of *what* to write. I had completed the (very) rough draft of a "mainstream" novel in Italy; should I go on with that? (Then I read it over and the answer came clear. It was very bad. I burned it.) My wife, Tina, was also a writer; should we collaborate? (We tried it, even actually finished a short Robert Nathan-y fantasy novel. I still have the manuscript, but have not had the courage to reread it in thirty years.) I had done some writing for the non-sf pulps before the war; since science fiction was not a very active market, should I do more of that? (I did do a couple of detective and mystery stories for Street & Smith's *Detective Story*, the Toronto *Star Weekly* and others, but they weren't a lot of fun.)

And after a while I realized that science fiction, my first love, was still my best.

All three of these novellas were published in the years just after World War II. For most of that time I had a full-time job which, along with other complications, limited my writing time, so that these comprise almost all the science fiction I wrote from World War II until I began the first drafts of what turned into *The Space Merchants*.

I don't think they are very much like *The Space Merchants*—or like *Gateway* or *The Gold at the Starbow's End* or, indeed, like almost anything else I have written since. They are space opera. They are action science fiction, meant for an action-oriented audience in the pulp magazines.

That statement is not meant to excuse them. For what they are, they are the best I was able to do. By the time I wrote them I had already made the decision to take writing seriously—which, among other things, meant that I had tried to break myself of the habit of writing and selling first drafts, so that each of these was rather extensively revised and rewritten before it was published.

Now when science fiction is published, it gets extensively reviewed and criticized. An author may quarrel with what critics say, and even bleed a little. But he is in no doubt about what people think of what he writes. In the late 1940s no one paid that much attention to science fiction. The only feedback a writer had came from the letter columns in science-fiction magazines, which is why all of us so avidly prowled the newsstands a month or two after each story came out. What the readers said now blurs in the memory; I remember that Theodore Sturgeon called *Donovan Had a Dream* "compelling action adventure," but I don't remember much else. For those reasons, and more, it is hard for me to know how to rate *Figurehead*, *Donovan Had a Dream* and *Red Moon of Danger* at this late date . . .

So I will leave the verdict up to you.

—Frederik Pohl

Red Bank, New Jersey
July, 1979

PLANETS THREE

Besides suggesting the right way to choose a pen name to me, John Campbell suggested all sorts of other things—now and then even a story idea. One of the ideas was of a race of intelligent beings who did not SEEM intelligent.

It was not a very completely worked out idea, and, besides, he was not suggesting it only to me. John did not believe on wasting an idea on a single writer. He usually gave the same idea to several—and frequently bought all the stories that came back, since he could reliably expect each writer to so shape it to his own skills that the common origin would be undetectable. In this case, it was an idea that he had used himself, in one of the Penton and Blake stories, years before.

But it was still an interesting idea, and I went home and tried to figure it into a story. It wasn't easy. And, worse than that, I am a slow writer. I've published a lot, but then I spend a lot of time writing—almost always several hours each day. So I worked on FIGUREHEAD for a while, then put it away to work on something else, then came back to it, and by the time I went into the Air

1

Force it was still incomplete. After the war I came back to it again, and actually managed to tease it all together in a shape that satisfied me . . . but by then John was no longer interested, and I ultimately sold it to Robert A. W. Lowndes.

Speaking of whom, it is about time I said in public something that I have known in my heart for many years. Bob Lowndes is one of the great unrecognized editors in science fiction. Throughout his career he was hampered by a reluctant publisher and the lowest of rates of pay, and nevertheless he managed to attract to his magazines some of the finest science-fiction writers with some of the best of their work. Personal charm and friendship accounted for part of that. The rest was patience, energy, wisdom and skill.

Figurehead

1

Duncan and I were almost there before they took us out of the paralysis.

We had no way of telling how long we had been in the ship, unconscious and unable to move, but I was sure it had been a long, long time. I ached in every muscle, and when I moved I was sure I could actually hear myself creak.

The little pink man who called himself the Boss was watching when we woke up out of our dazed condition. "Don't make trouble," he advised us at once in his excited clipped tones. He carefully displayed a rod-like affair that I was willing to concede was a gun—though it might as well have been a pearl-handled backscratcher. His English was amazingly good, considering that he was nowhere near human. He looked like a toad that was ambitious to become a leprechaun.

"Don't make trouble," he repeated, and: "It won't get you anywhere. Since you're awake I suppose you'll want to ask questions. Go ahead. I won't answer them, probably."

I looked at him and sat down on the hygienic, slightly

resilient slab I'd been using for a bed. Questions? Sure I had questions, but what were they? Duncan got in first. "Why did you wake us up?" he asked with more objectivity than I owned. "Wouldn't it have been easier to keep us the way we were?"

"No. You were a damned nuisance. So was he." The last was accompanied by a webby, three-fingered gesture at me. I spoke up.

"What are you going to do with us?"

The pink imp leered. "You'll find out."

"When? And where are we going?"

"I won't tell you. I told you I probably wouldn't answer your questions. All you specimens ask the same things. It's none of your business." The toad-imp was frowning.

I shrugged and became practical. What he said didn't seem to matter very much, anyhow—possibly I was still under a hangover from the trancelike state we'd been in. "When do we eat?" I asked.

For the first time, the Boss stopped to think about a question. It occurred to me that he actually looked alarmed. He drew a thing like a lady's compact from the pouch he wore at his waist and flipped it open.

"Tomorrow," he announced with a glint of relief in his voice, after he had looked inside. "You get one meal before we land. Now you've asked enough questions. I won't answer any more. If there's anything you need, you can shout for it. Make sure you need it," he added sinisterly.

And he left, through a rather circular sort of door.

Duncan sat down on his bed and looked at me. He said, "What do you think, Nick?"

I shrugged. I didn't know what to think. It was all pretty confusing.

Not so long before, life had been very simple. There was Duncan and there was I, and there was broad green water all around us and a little rubber life raft bouncing under us. There were no complications. All we had to do was reach land before we starved to death or overturned and drowned. Very simple.

As simple and natural as a Gulf Stream hurricane. When our cabin cruiser swamped and went down, I went down with it. By the grace of the good lord and the personal intercession of my patron saint, sometimes known as Santa Claus, I came up again close enough to Duncan and his life raft to clutch a thrown rope. The third member of our party, Tommy Cleelock, and the other life raft were nowhere in sight—which was true of anything more than twenty yards away, in that storm. We drifted all night. About noon the next day we saw a plane way off on the horizon, and a plume of smoke under it. There was no way of attracting their attention; we didn't even try. I like to think that they were looking for us, but as Duncan points out that was impossible; nobody would think of missing us for at least a week.

But a bit later we saw the loom of land.

We paddled toward it. We beached the life raft about an hour before dusk the second day, the hottest day of that or any year.

Everything was still and steaming hot. There was a malarial-looking jungle creeping down practically to the water line, but if there was any wild life in it, it was hiding. An unpleasantly muddy greenish stream was seeping along mouldy ground, burying itself in the sand at the jungle's edge.

We didn't like the looks of it for drinking purposes, but thought it might be clearer near its source. So we struck into the heart of that deathly quiet jungle.

We found the end of our trip before we found the source of that brackish stream. Our life raft, for all I know, might still be on the beach, unless the tide took it away. Though the little people more likely collapsed it and carried it off with them, the same time they took us; they were insufferably curious. I think that was the reason they had been promoted to the status of intelligence. With them, you see, evolution was not an abstract issue that two lawyers could debate in a courtroom. They knew about it, because they'd been through it themselves . . .

Anyway, we never found the source—because the little people found us first.

All the way up the stream we had the sensation of being followed. Finally, after looking furtively over our shoulders had showed us nothing; we just stood stock-still and waited.

It brought results.

There was a scrabbling in the underbrush and shrill, muted voices whispering musically about something. Then three little pink creatures—I've described the Boss; they all look about alike—hopped out of the jungle.

"Do not be afraid, men," one called to us. It wasn't what he said; it was sheer surprise at the looks of them that kept us from fighting them off, until it was too late. Before we collected ourselves we had been jabbed with tiny needles. There was a sharp pang, like a wasp's sting—

And, like a wasp's prey, we were paralyzed.

We stayed that way until they woke us up. Part of the time we were at least semi-conscious, because I remember one or two things in a hazy sort of way. The pink ones examining us, jabbing us with more needles, systematically disrobing us and then tossing the clothes back on us helter-skelter. I remember meeting the boss at one point—he was the English-speaking one—and being told that he gave the orders around there; we were to hop to it when he gave us any. He told us that himself.

And I remember being carried to a burned-out clearing where there rested a huge purplish torpedo of a ship—a rocket, in fact. We were dragged into it and put in a room, on a pair of soft, shock-absorbing pads. A pink one stuck his toad's head in the door a minute later to see that we were all right. And pretty soon thereafter there was a hell of a bang right below us and we felt sudden, sharp pressure.

The ship had taken off.

It seemed like a few days or weeks elapsed while we

lay quiescent on those pads. Actually, I discovered later, it was a bit more than eighteen months!

I got around to answering Duncan's question with a question of my own.

"Where do you suppose we are?" I asked. "What goes on?"

Duncan grinned. He said, "That bespeaks immense faith in me, Nick. I'm sorry to let you down, but I don't know."

"Well, let's figure it out logically," I started, but Duncan halted me with a shake of the head. "There's no logic involved," he said. "The whole thing's screwy. I'm here, and I know I'm not dreaming, but I find it hard to believe all the same. Why don't we try the empirical method, Nick, and look around? Have you noticed"—he gestured—"that the door's not closed?"

I stared at it. It was open all right, just a crack. I walked over to it, and was suddenly conscious of the fact that I had lost weight. I don't mean that I had lost fat; I hate euphemisms. I had the same mass as ever, but the acceleration of the ship, evidently, was less than one Earth gravity. By rough feel, I weighed perhaps a hundred pounds. A little less than two-thirds normal.

I stepped lightly to keep on the floor, conscious of a curious surge beneath me that was the throbbing of the rocket jets, and touched the door. It slid open all the way as soon as I laid my hand on it. I looked out, with Duncan breathing hotly on my shoulder.

"I can't see anything," Duncan said disappointedly. "Look, Nick, let's take a walk."

"You think we ought to? The Boss wouldn't like it."

Outside the door was a corridor, metal-walled, floored with the same rubbery red stuff that was on the floor of our room. To our left it intersected with another corridor just like it, about five yards from us. To our right it ran a bit farther, then made a sharp bend; there were no other doors visible than the one we were leaning out of.

"I don't care what the Boss would like," Duncan said. "He didn't order us to stay here."

He broke off and listened. "Voices," he said excitedly. "Somebody's coming!"

I am a cautious man, so I grabbed the sleeve of Duncan's jacket and pulled him back into the room. I am also curious; I did not close the door.

I was glad that I hadn't closed it. The voices got louder—only it wasn't "voices". There was just one voice, a girl's. She was singing to herself quietly, the way you do when there's no one around to hear you. She wasn't singing in English, or in the kind of tonal music you hear over the radio. It was a liquid sort of language, totally incomprehensible, and the music flowed liquidly also. There were no breaks in it, no jump from note to note, but only a smooth flow. You could play music like that very well on a musical saw—or on the electronic gadget they call a theramin.

"Pretty voice," said Duncan, and I took a better grip on the sleeve of his gunner's tunic. "I hope *she* is as pretty—"

Then she passed the door, she and her . . . well, it looked like it was her pet; a great big shaggy dog that walked on its hind legs. It wore a thick metal collar around its ugly neck, and there was blankness and idiocy in its eyes. A hideous thing, all hairy and unpleasant, as big as a man.

She was not hideous. Neither was she human, I thought; probably it would have been too much to have expected a human girl there. But she was close enough . . .

I believe she was the most beautiful girl I ever saw. Tall and slender, but neatly and in fact sumptuously rounded where roundness is needful; vividly gorgeous of face. There was a height to her cheekbones and a quirk to the ends of her lips; a sort of hazy tilt to her eyes—Slavic, I thought she looked. I wonder how a Slav would have described her.

All that was human enough—or superhuman. It was

her hair that wasn't; it literally floated around her head, spider-silk thin and weightless. It was long and glistening, a pale pink corona that swirled and danced lazily as she walked. Quite a thing. Quite a damnably gorgeous thing, that any woman on Earth would have given half a lifetime to own.

I thought Duncan spoke to me. "Don't bother me," I said, keeping my eyes on the girl. "Tell me about it later."

"I didn't say anything," he protested. "I thought *you* spoke."

That disconcerted me enough to turn around and look at him. "Somebody spoke," I said; "somebody a long way off, maybe."

"That's what I heard," he nodded. Puzzled, I tried to reconstruct the feeling. It was a voice, I was sure, but I had no idea what it had been saying. But it didn't seem particularly important, and Duncan interrupted the thought.

"Hey," he said. "Front and center Nick. She's giving us the once-over."

She had stopped and turned around, and now she was looking at us, her lips still parted but no longer singing.

"Hello," said Duncan tentatively.

Her face grimaced involuntarily, as though she were repelled by the sound of his voice. But she controlled it and, after a moment, the frown vanished. Instead, her lips parted again and rich music came out, mocking music.

She was laughing at us.

"A fine reception we're getting, I must say," Duncan said disgustedly. "Lady, don't you know any better manners than that?"

Apparently she didn't because, still laughing, she turned around and left. We watched her pace slowly to the intersection, with that shaggy brute shambling along beside her, a silvery wire leash running from his collar to what looked like a similar collar around her own neck. She turned to the right and kept on walking, still singing. We listened to her voice die away. I wish I could make that melody into a symphony. It deserves it.

"Wow!" said Duncan, and he turned to look at me. I had never seen Duncan wide-eyed before; it was not an attractive sight. "I begin to like this place," he said. "I hope she's a permanent guest."

There was a squeal of high-pitched indignation from behind us. "Hey!" shouted a shrill voice. "What do you think you're doing?"

We spun around involuntarily. It was the Boss, racing down the corridor toward us with all boilers blazing and a deckhand sitting on the safety valve. "Get back in your cage!" he yelled. "You're not allowed out. Move!"

We moved, hurriedly. Greatly daring, Duncan said, "Who was that we just saw?"

The Boss' face took on a peculiar look that seemed almost like reverence. "The Khreen," he said.

"She's a pretty girl," Duncan commented. "Can we see her again?"

"Girl?" he asked scornfully. "Sure. She doesn't matter; she's just another specimen. You'll see plenty of her."

Duncan protested, "But you said she was—"

"Never mind what I said," the Boss interrupted, glaring at us from the doorway. "Now you stay here. If you want to get in trouble, just come out again. Big trouble, from me personally."

Duncan shrugged. "Why?" he asked reasonably. "We've been in here a long time. We're getting tired of it—and hungry, besides."

The Boss' glare faded a little and took on a sickly tinge. "You should complain," he said morosely, but didn't complete the thought. "I told you when you'd get fed. Tomorrow."

"Be seeing you then," I said.

The Boss' frog face split in a sardonic, unhappy grin. "That," he said, "is only too true." And he slid the door back, with a faint click we hadn't heard before. When Duncan tried it experimentally a little later, we found it was locked.

"Oh, well," he said. "We're not supposed to anyhow." He poked the resilient slab on his side of the room with a finger, then sprawled out on it.

"We might as well get some sleep," he said.

I followed his example, but I had a puzzlement in my mind that wanted settling. Before I fell asleep I said, "What do you suppose is biting on the Boss?"

Duncan, his back to me, shrugged. "No idea at all," he said. "Go to sleep. He'll probably tell you all about it, in his sour fashion, when we see him tomorrow."

2

But when we saw the Boss again he was in high spirits. "I like you," he said happily as soon as he was in the door. "Look—food."

He displayed two hunks of dripping meat one in each webbed hand. He gave them to us and said, "Go ahead and eat; I'll watch you."

I took mine rather gingerly and gave it a thorough inspection. It had not been cooked, apparently, but it was quite warm. I sniffed it and liked what I smelled, so I took a nibble.

I've tasted worse. It was odd, but edible. If you fed a pig on herring for a couple of months before slaughtering him, then smoked the hams in the fumes of Chinese incense, it might taste like that. It wasn't unbearably bad, once you got used to it.

Finding the Boss in a good humor was so unexpected that we didn't take advantage of it for a while. When I'd finished gnawing on my chunk of meat I broke the conversational ice. "Why wouldn't you let us look out the door yesterday?" I asked tentatively. "Was it that girl? Is she tabu or something?"

He grinned, but amiably. "I won't tell you. Don't you know that I'll tell you hardly anything?"

"I'm beginning to find out," I agreed, quite sincerely.

His face clouded as though I had hurt his feelings. He said, "I'll tell you one thing, because I like you. Today we land. This is the end of our voyage—and I've finished another trip alive!"

I gaped at him. He was positively beamish over his triumph of survival, grinning to himself like a moon-struck leprechaun. "Shall I show you something?" he whispered conspiratorially. "Something you'd like to see? I oughtn't to do it, but it doesn't matter. And I like you. Shall I show you?"

"Sure," said Duncan. I nodded eagerly.

"All right," said the Boss. He opened the door, stepped out into the corridor. "Come on," he said.

We followed him, Duncan and I. We turned to the right at the door, followed along the corridor to where it made its sharp bend to the left, then walked a few paces along the new corridor. He stopped before a door and craned his thick neck anxiously to look at us.

"Do you know why I like you?" he asked suddenly. "It is not because of anything you did. You are rather loathesome to me, you know. Oh, it's not your fault; all of you specimens are basically revolting, when you come right down to it. You can't help it . . . I like you," he said, "because you do not eat very much."

He grinned happily. "You don't understand?" he said in high good humor. "Of course you don't; you weren't expected to. Now, we will go in here. Conduct yourselves well, because I will kill you if you get me in trouble. I would have no compunctions. I don't like you *very* well."

With a grand gesture he flung the door open and motioned us in.

We found ourselves in a large room. It was filled with some of the most fantastic hunks of gadgetry you'll see in a month of Whitsuntides. "Jeepers," said Duncan, and it expressed my feelings perfectly.

There were machines in the room . . . but such machines as I had never come across before. Little ones and big ones; square ones and one that seemed to be made out of odds and ends of runny tar and crepe paper—shapeless.

One of the gadgets dominated the entire thirty-foot room. It would have dominated any room. It was quite sensational.

There was a shallow tank of an orange liquid, rectangular, with a fountain coming up out of the middle. It was decorative—a curious flashing jet of brilliant orange—but its function was not merely decoration. For there was a small group standing in the pool, two or three pinkies, a couple of the dog-beasts, and the girl.

"What a way to take a shower," Duncan breathed over my shoulder.

That's what it looked like. From the falling orange spray, from the jet of the fountain itself, from the surface of the pool, droplets of what looked like pure radiant energy were forming, drifting about and dropping back to the pool. Fat orange sparks, that weren't electricity because they didn't crackle or spit, just collected and floated lazily around and down. Where they were drifting the thickest, there stood the pinkies and their companions, standing there with eyes closed and expressions of seraphic rapture on their faces, letting the sparks, or whatever, soak into them.

I heard the Boss puffing contentedly beside me. "What is it?" I asked him. "What are they doing?"

It was a stupid question, of course, because I knew what his answer would be. "I won't tell you," he said delightedly. "Anyway, that's not what I brought you here to see. I wanted—Hey! Come back!"

He was talking to Duncan's back. Duncan's front, followed by the rest of Duncan, was heading purposefully toward the tank, and the girl.

The Boss shrieked in pure rage and jumped for Duncan. He leaped on his back, dragging him back toward me. I stood paralyzed. Duncan grunted,

"What—what's the matter," half choked by the Boss' throttling arm.

"Animal! Beast! I told you to obey orders! It is death for you if you touch the life-waters!" He released Duncan and jumped back, panting heavily, his hand close to the paralysis needle he carried in his belt.

Duncan shrugged. "All right," he said; "I just wanted to talk to the girl."

"Talk! Hah! You couldn't understand her. You think our people bother to learn your stupid tongue?"

"You did," Duncan pointed out. "Besides, you said she was a specimen too. From Earth, like us, I take it?"

The Boss snorted. Aggrievedly he said, "Never mind about her. This is what I get for being good to you. Animals!"

"Sorry," said Duncan in resignation. "Lead on, Boss."

He scowled blackly, then jerked his thumb to the far corner of the room. "Over there," he said bitterly.

In the corner was another door. We marched over to it—or glided might be a better word, because our Earth-trained strides gave us an odd bounce at every step in the light drag. The Boss flung the door open.

"Look inside," he ordered, his tone becoming more calm.

We looked. The sparks from the tank were drifting about and, though they weren't very dense, it was strangely hard to see through an atmosphere that was all cluttered up with fat, luminescent hunks of orangeness. Where they were thickest it was like trying to look down into the waters off Bermuda on a muggy August night when a boat has just stirred up the plankton.

But I looked, and I saw, finally, who it was that was sitting there, staring at me with a curiously angry expression on his face. I might not have recognized him at first, but he said, "Hi-ya, palsies," and that clinched it. It was Tommy Cleelock, raised from the dead.

"But he was drowned," Duncan objected. I shook my head.

"Not Tommy," I told him. "He'll never drown. Born to hang."

Cleelock got up and walked over to us. "So they got you too," he observed, and I saw that he was white-lipped. His voice was taut, too, though his words were easy enough.

"Surprised to see us, Tommy?" I asked inanely. "Well, we're surprised—"

"Nah," he said; "they told me you were alive. Didn't know you were on this ship, but I had a pretty good idea you might be."

"Oh," I said. There was a brief silence. Then Duncan said: "Well, *I'm* surprised. What are *you* doing here?"

"Same thing you are," he told us.

"How do you like being a human sacrifice?"

"Human sacrifice?"

Tommy grinned mirthlessly, jerked a thumb at the Boss. "Ask him?"

The Boss frowned. "You are making trouble," he accused. "You specimens will not be hurt; you are wanted only for research."

"Sure, research. Like vivisection, for instance."

The Boss tossed his head and didn't deign to answer.

"Look," I said earnestly to Tommy, "tell me more about this. I want to know what you're talking about."

"Oh, it's nothing," Tommy said morosely. "Just don't count on ever seeing home again, that's all. We're going to Ganymede."

"Ganymede? What's Ganymede?"

"Ganymede," Tommy explained, "is one of the moons of Jupiter. The planet. That's where we're going."

"Oh," I said. I will say for myself that I took that calmly enough—after all, the signs had been pointed straight to something of the sort. "Uh—why Ganymede?" I asked.

"Because that's where he comes from." Tommy pointed again to the Boss.

The Boss nodded, grinning widely. "Naturally, I come from Ganymede," he said superiorly. "You didn't think Mars, did you? You thought maybe people lived on Mars, that dry old place? Ho-ho-ho! Stupid!''

"All right," I said pacifically. "Anyway, what I'm interested in is—what happens to us when we get there?"

Tommy said earnestly, "If I knew the answer to that, I'd sell you the information at a million dollars a word. That character"— he pointed again at the Boss—"gives double talk, exclusively."

"You'll find out," the Boss said cryptically. He yawned, showing a mouth full of randomly spaced teeth. "I leave you for a while," he announced, and closed the door from outside. Apparently he was going over to chat with his spark-bathing friends.

Tommy shook his head mournfully. "To think I taught him everything he knows," he observed. "Gratitude!"

"What did you teach him?" I asked.

"Everything!" He leaned back against a bulkhead and looked sad. "I lost you, see, during the storm. I see Duncan go off with the stern life raft, and I drag the other one out of the cabin. I get it into the drink and fall in with it, and the next thing I see of anything but water, I'm drifting onto this island. I go ashore and wander around. Everything goes fine, until all of a sudden I see things moving. It's these little pink devils. One of them sneaks up on me, and stabs me when I'm not looking, and—*zap*, I'm out like a light." He glared at me.

"I didn't do it," I protested hastily. "What then?"

"Well—" he scratched his head. "Then come things I don't understand. I wake up, and I'm in this thing, which according to the Boss is a rocket ship. Only he doesn't tell me this at that time, because at that time he doesn't speak any English. So I teach it to him."

"You do—I mean, you did?" I thought it over. "We've been gone longer than I thought, maybe. His grammar stinks, but it's no worse than yours. Must have taken him months to learn it."

Tommy shook his head. "Don't interrupt," he said. "First, you're right; we've been gone longer than you thought. Don't know how long, but it's months—the Boss told me. Second, it didn't take him long to learn English. All I did was talk. He caught on like a knitted sweater in a barbed-wire fence. He sat there in my cell, with his pet baboon scratching fleas next to him, watching me until I got nervous. Then he began pointing to things. I'm no dope; I got the idea quick. I told him the names of everything in sight, and acted out a couple of simple verbs, and by and by all I had to do was answer his questions. Amazing."

"How long did it take?" I asked curiously.

"You won't believe me."

"How long?"

He sighed. "Two days."

I straightened up and gave him the eye. "Cleelock," I said, "you're a cockeyed liar."

He shrugged without resentment. "I told you," he reminded me. "I wouldn't have believed it either. But the little son never forgot a thing. It was terrific. I guess he doesn't believe in sleep, or something—I passed out twice the first day, still talking, before he would believe that I had to get a little rest. Yammer, yammer, yammer. I never heard so much talking in my life. We talked about everything under the sun." He shook his head. "He asked more questions than the Internal Revenue bureau. I—I had an idea somebody was helping him with his homework, if you get what I mean. Suggesting questions to him, helping him figure out the answers. But there wasn't anybody else in the room."

"Did he tell you anything about what they plan to do with us?"

"A couple of things. He said we were going to Ganymede, and, no, I'd never go back. He said something that sounded very unpleasant about surgical tests—then he clammed up." A troubled look came into Cleelock's eyes. Slowly he said, "One funny thing he told me—I don't get it, exactly. I was describing a dog to him. He got all excited, then he decided that *he* was a dog."

"Huh," I said. "Maybe he meant he was an animal."

"No, I don't think so—at least, not exactly. Later on I began on class nouns. He let 'animal' go by without an objection, but when I came to 'pet', he decided he was one of those. You know what that means?"

I thought it over. "Pet," I said. "You mean he's just a domestic animal?"

Cleelock spread his palms. "You know as much as I do," he said. "But that's the impression I got—except that, if they don't run their planet, who does?"

Duncan, with his jaw hanging, snapped it shut and nodded wisely. "The girl," he said.

I said, "No—not according to the Boss. Remember? He said she was a specimen like us."

Cleelock brushed me off. "Girl?" he asked. "What girl?"

"Why, the redhead in the corridor. The slick-chick soprano."

But Tommy hadn't seen the girl at all. When we finished telling him about her he was all excited. "This might not be so bad, hey?" he said, his eyes glittering. "She sounds like a knockout."

Before I could think of a good squelching remark the Boss came back. "Visit's over," he said, staring in at us through the door. "We go back to your cage."

Tommy glared at him. "I could dislike you," he said. Then, significantly, "I'm getting a little hungry, by the way."

The Boss flinched. "You are not," he protested feebly; "you just ate."

I asked, "What's the gag?"

"Don't you know?" Cleelock laughed in somber glee. "It's the only thing we've got on these characters. Have you eaten yet?"

"Why, sure."

"What did you have?"

I was puzzled. "Some kind of meat; it was raw, but it tasted all right."

Cleelock nodded superiorly. "Know what it was?" he asked.

"No." I looked curiously at the Boss, who seemed

acutely unhappy. Then I got it, and gasped. "You mean that meat—"

"Yep," said Tommy. "What you ate was a piece of pink devil. It's the only kind of food they carry."

3

I gave up eating for the rest of the trip. Fortunately, that was only a matter of a few hours, but the way I felt I never wanted to eat again anyhow. The Boss wasn't exactly my own race, but he spoke English and seemed intelligent . . . and cannibalism had never appealed to me.

Duncan and I talked it over rather unhappily, and came to no important conclusion. It seemed so revoltingly impossible—but the Boss hadn't denied it.

We let it go, and lay back on our slabs to brood over the whole thing. A couple hours after we left Tommy Cleelock the Boss came into our cubbyhole and ordered us to stay on the slabs. Then he departed, and presently we felt the ship begin to slam around as though it were being jockeyed in for a landing—which, obviously, it was. There was one final jolt, and a bump, and the throbbing of the engines died.

The Boss and one of his pink helpers trotted in. They prodded us down the corridor to the exit hatch, picking up Tommy Cleelock on the way.

We came out onto a landscape with a lavender sky.

"So this is Ganymede," Duncan breathed. "Flat, isn't it?"

I agreed with him. There wasn't a mountain in sight. Maybe time and erosion did it—Ganymede, I found out later, is an ancient, ancient world—or maybe it was that way to begin with. But the only thing that broke the level of the horizon was a group of immense spires maybe fifteen miles away.

Duncan pointed to it. He said, "That looks like a pretty big city. Bigger than New York even, maybe."

"Maybe," said Cleelock derisively. "Those buildings are a good mile high."

"Come on, come on," the Boss said in his peevish, high-pitched voice. "Don't keep us waiting." I looked behind us, and the Boss had been joined by a couple more pinkies, convoying the gorgeous girl and her beast. A couple more pinkies were trotting around the corridors on what seemed to be urgent errands, but I didn't bother to watch them. I was looking at the girl.

I took a good look at her, and by the fact that Cleelock was breathing hard I could tell that he was doing the same. Nearby and in daylight, she was prettier than I had imagined. I could see, though, that she was not the human being I'd taken her for. What the Boss said about her being a specimen like us crossed my mind, but I brushed it aside. Like us she was not. Her whole build was too delicate, too slight for humanity and the pinkish aurelle that hung about her head was much too fine to be the hair of a human.

"I said come *on*," snapped the Boss, and nudged us toward a thing on wheels. It was more like a canoe than a car, but we got in, all of us, and the pinky who sat in front fiddled with some push-buttons and the car began to move. It was headed off at a right angle from the direction of the city, and I was about to say something about it, when we rounded the stern of the purple rocket. I saw another city spread before us.

But it wasn't much of a city.

I took a quick look at the one behind us for comparison. There was no comparison. When the one on the horizon was tall and slender, this one was squat and ugly. The one was a spiry fairyland of towers; the other an alphabet-block collection of cubes.

"Wouldn't you know it?" murmured Cleelock. "We end up in a Ganymedan slum."

"Shut up," the Boss said petulantly. I stole a look at him. His unpredictable mood had changed again; where a couple of hours before he had been almost affable, now he was his customary surly self.

The car skidded as the driver twirled a little rod, and came round in an arc to head for the nearest of the cubes. I could see at close range, that the buildings hadn't even windows to recommend them—nothing but a blank facade of what looked like cheap stucco.

"Maybe they'll let us live in the rocket," Duncan suggested. "This place doesn't look like home to me."

The car skidded to a stop before our destined cube and, on orders from the Boss, we hopped out and walked inside. We all three had to bend over to enter, because the frame of the door was cut for someone about five feet four or less. Inside, the ceilings were a uniform six feet above the floor, a fact which I deduced from the angle at which six-foot-one Tommy Cleelock's head was bent.

We were assailed by a loud metallic clanging. "What the devil," Cleelock said. "What's that noise?"

We listened. "Air pumps, maybe?" I guessed. It was a rhythmic clash, and it sounded like air pumps if it sounded like anything at all. But so loud!

"Fine," said Duncan in complete disgust. "What do you make of that? These people build terrific rocket ships, but when it comes to a simple thing like an air-conditioning system they fall flat on their faces. I never heard so much noise."

"Maybe they like noise," I guessed; "maybe they don't care."

Before we could carry the conversation any further the witch-girl interrupted. Staring at us, she trilled something musical—not to us, but almost as though she

were just light-heartedly bursting into song. But there
was an answer from the Boss. He ripped off a brief
burst of melody—I thought that, compared to her, he
was a little flat—and then scowled at me.

"Do you specimens need to sleep now?" he asked
gruffly.

I looked at the others, who seemed rested enough. I
said, "No."

"How about eating?"

"Well—" I hesitated over the answer. "If it's true
about eating *you*—"

He winced. "That was only on the ship," he said
hastily. "Here we have other things—plants, or something. Whatever you specimens usually eat."

"That would be fine," I said.

We ate pale blue, thick-stemmed ferns. They were
peppery, but the Boss snapped pettishly that they were
all right. "Better than you deserve," he added.
"Anyway, you won't have to worry about eating much
longer, probably—" a remark which I considered in
notoriously bad taste.

Duncan chopped off a fern stem with a dull flat knife
they had given us and stared at the girl. She was
standing near us, day-dreaming. Apparently she didn't
bother to eat any more than the rest of this nightmare
bunch but Duncan tried offering her a piece of fern. It
got him but nowhere . . . she looked through, over and
beyond him, but never eye to eye. She wasn't avoiding
him deliberately; he just plain didn't make any impression.

"Where's her two-legged sheepdog?" Duncan asked
suddenly. Reminded, I looked around, but the animal
wasn't in the room.

Cleelock volunteered, "The Boss took it out for a
walk. Didn't you see? The gal had a collar around her
neck, attached to the leash. She took it off, and the Boss
put it on, and the two of them walked out, him and the
beast." He chuckled. "That's a terrific arrangement
they have," he commented. "Both the Boss and the dog

wear collars when they go out walking—you can hardly tell which is master and which is dog.''

When the Boss came back, he had the animal with him sure enough and both wore the flat silvery collars.

The Boss said, in a tone that was new and surprising simply because it was tranquil, "Come along with us, all three of you." He looked at the girl and a ripple of music came from his batrachian lips. She trilled a reply, showing interest in the proceedings for the first time, and he turned and led us out of the room.

In the hall, the raucous clangor of the air pumps was twice as bad as in the room where we had been fed. We faced it with gritted teeth and allowed ourselves to be conducted to what looked to be an elevator. We all got in, the Boss pushed a button and closed the door; a second's wait and the door opened.

"Well," said Cleelock. "Things are looking up. I like their no-jar elevators."

I nodded. After their unpleasantly inefficient air-conditioning, this latest taste of Ganymedan technology had been a pleasant surprise. There hadn't been a hint of jolting or motion, yet now we were looking out on another corridor, this one broad and well-lighted.

The Boss led the way. He took us to a large room that looked like, and turned out to be, a surgery.

"Hey," said Cleelock in an alarmed tone. "Boss, what are you planning to do here?"

"Test you," the Boss said. "Sit down."

"Test us for what?"

The Boss shrugged—or tried to shrug; his shoulders were of about the same dimensions as his neck, and all he achieved was a sort of twitch. "To see what we can do with you, of course," he said. He pointed to the red-head. "For instance, we might give you the treatment we gave her."

I looked at the girl. Whatever the "treatment" was, she didn't seem in terribly bad shape. Extra *good* shape, in fact, I would have said. But still—

"What's the treatment like?" I asked. "What did you do to her? Was she like us once?"

"Like you? No. She was female. And much smaller."

"But what did you do to her?" I begged.

Placidly the Boss waved a hand. "What we did to her," he said serenely, "was what was done once to all of us. She came from your dirty little planet, and was captured as a specimen. She was very tiny. There were others with her." He looked us over speculatively. "About the size of you, they were," he said. "They died."

"Awk," I said involuntarily. I covered up with a question. "Do you have many specimens from our planet?" I asked.

"No. Just you three. And her."

"What did—I mean, what did the others die of?"

He smiled benignly. "Various things," he said.

"Now, look, Boss—" Cleelock started to get up and remonstrate. The Boss scowled.

"Sit down!" he said, and Cleelock sat down. More calmly, the Boss went on, "I will tell you a story to quiet your nerves. It begins here on Ganymede, just under a million of your years ago."

"I don't want a story," Cleelock protested. "I want—"

"I don't care what you want," the Boss said mildly but finally. "This story is about solitary confinement. Not one man in solitary confinement, though. A whole race."

Cleelock said, "How can a race be solitary, Boss?"

The Boss glared. "All right," he said angrily, "I won't tell you; I was against it anyhow."

Cleelock pulled in his horns. "Wait a minute, Boss. Let's—let's hear the story. Before you—test us. I mean."

The Boss shook his head. He pointed to the door. "Too late," he said ominously. "The examiners are ready."

We looked apprehensively at the door.

Three pinkies were coming in, each with a shaggy beast on a leash to keep him company. The foremost of them was struggling under a clumsy object that looked a little like an electric chair. He set it down, fussed with some gadgets on the back of it and looked at me expectantly. He sang a little song of invitation.

"All right," said the Boss—but to my relief, he was talking to Cleelock instead of me. "Sit down."

Cleelock dazedly stumbled over to the chair and sat, not with any appearance of comfort.

The Boss called something musical; the pinky by the chair touched something among the gadgets; there was a quick crackle of energy.

Cleelock's body became completely transparent. "Hey!" he squawked. "What's going on?"

"Oh, Tommy," I said. "You look funny. I can see right through you."

"Well, *I* can't see a thing." He was peering frantically around the room, his eyes like a blind man's. "Everything's all out of focus, like. What *is* this?"

"Your cornea doesn't refract," I started to say learnedly—but by the time I got the words out it didn't matter. The pinkies had conferred briefly in musical sounds, and the sound of energy died. Cleelock's body once more became opaque, and his naked skeleton was clothed with flesh.

"Take it away," he moaned. "I'll be good."

The Boss was gesturing to me and, there being no help for it, I took my place in the hot seat. When the juice came on it didn't fry me, as I had expected. In fact there was no sensation at all, except that peculiar inability to focus my vision that had troubled Cleelock. Everything ran lumpily together, and nothing looked like anything at all. Involuntarily I closed my eyes to shut out the sight. That was a gross error. It's bad enough seeing chaos with the eyes open. When your eyelids have become transparent, and you can feel them pressed tightly shut, and still you see a maelstrom of light and color, then it is bad.

But it didn't last. A few seconds, and I was replaced by Duncan. And a few more seconds and we were all through.

The Boss was talking things over with the three other pinkies. Then he turned to us, his face registering dissatisfaction.

"How'd we come out, Boss?" I asked hopefully.

"Hah," he said darkly. "No good."

"No good?"

"No. You are too old; we cannot give you the treatment. That means only one thing," he added, scowling darkly. "There must be purification!" And he pointed to the door with a theatrical gesture.

We trooped out as he directed, back to the elevator. Inside he pressed another of the buttons, and the door closed and opened as before. "What do you make of this 'purification' business?" whispered Cleelock. "Sounds bad to me."

But before I could answer the door was open again, and bright sunlight was streaming in.

We looked out onto what seemed to be a roof garden. I gathered, from our position about forty feet from the edge of it, that it was no small roof, either. To judge by the way the horizon looked we were a good thousand feet in the air.

We were standing on a path made of translucent, reddish stone. All about us grew bushes and trees.

"Come along," said the Boss, mildly enough, and pointed to a pond. We walked ahead of him, and I stared down into it.

Whatever it was, it wasn't water. It was the same stuff I had seen in the fountain back on the ship—a livid orange liquid with all the appearance of fire. A still, limpid flame, so vivid that I expected heat and was surprised when there was none.

"Whaddya know," exclaimed Cleelock. "A fishpond of Martinis!"

The Boss marched up beside us and, benignly resting a hand on the sloping shoulder of his faithful beast, addressed us.

"Jump in," he said.

"*What?*"

Pettishly, "Jump in!"

Cleelock said determinedly, "No. Look, Boss, that stuff's dangerous. How do we know what it is? Maybe it's acid."

The little ridges of muscle where the Boss' eyebrows should have been went up. "You refuse to jump?" he asked incredulously.

"Well, yes." Cleelock stood his ground.

The Boss turned to me. "Jump in!"

"I'd—I'd rather not."

And Duncan chimed in, "Me too. I don't see the sense in it."

The girl, who had been watching us wide-eyed, sang something questioning and rapid to the Boss, who gave her a quick arpeggio in return. To us he said, "You don't have any choice, you specimens; you must go in the pool. It is for the purification. Besides, I tell you to!"

"Huh-uh." Cleelock shook his head vigorously, Duncan and I backing him up. "Be reasonable, Boss. That stuff looks kind of deadly."

I expected the Boss to tear into a tantrum but he merely glowered indecisively for a moment, then ripped off a many-noted bugle call in the general direction of the bushes. There was a moment of waiting, then half a dozen pinkies appeared. The Boss, scowling at us, sang them a catchy little air that boded us no good.

Like football players getting ready for a line buck, they formed a wedge and advanced on us, edging us closer to the pool.

"Wait a minute," Duncan begged. "Look, Boss, we're the specimens you like. Remember? We don't eat much."

"In the pool," snarled the Boss. "Jump!"

The three of us were huddled together, giving ground slowly and unwillingly. Cleelock, next to me, swore under his breath. "Okay, Nick," he whispered. "He's asking for it. When I jump for the Boss, you grab the girl. Duncan—you take one of the others. Any one. Got it?"

"Huh?" I asked stupidly, but I felt his hand prodding something into mind. It was flat and coldly metallic, and I found out—the hard way—that it had a sharp edge. It was one of the knives they'd given us to eat with! Cleelock had been smarter than either Duncan or me—he'd thought to snatch the knives for a future emergency!

"Jump!" the Boss said coldly again, and the other pinkies came on toward us. We retreated until there was nothing behind us but pool. Then—

"Now!" roared Cleelock, and sprang for the Boss. A split second behind him, I grabbed the girl, held the knife to her flimsily covered torso. She shrieked a terrified coloratura aria, the Boss squawked in surprise and Cleelock bellowed: "Now we'll see who's running things! Boss, call off your dogs—or we'll puncture your gizzard!"

The pinkies froze in consternation. For a moment it looked as though we had the situation well under control, but it didn't last. The Boss frothed:

"You foolish men! There are too many of us—you must go in the pool!" And he shrieked something in their polytonal tongue, and the other pinkies came on.

Cleelock wavered and Duncan and I watched him for our cue. Then he cursed furiously and threw down his knife. "Hit that line!" he bellowed, and lunged into the knot of pinkies.

Duncan and I piled into them after him. It could have been slaughter if we had used the knives, but we didn't have to. Their childlike, light-gravity bodies were like straws in our way.

We hurled them aside, boiled through and bounded for the elevator cage, Cleelock showing the way. Surprise and the simple business of picking themselves up from where we'd thrown them kept the pinkies a reasonable distance behind us, and Cleelock had time to fumble around with the buttons. He chose one at random, poked it . . .

It worked! The door slid shut. There was a brief

pause; it opened again. No jolt, no lurch, no jar . . . but we were no longer on the roof. We were looking out into a pitch-black corridor.

Cleelock poked his head out tentatively. Nothing happened; we all stepped out, looked up and down. Utter blackness, not a fleck of light anywhere, except what came from the elevator itself.

"Now what?" whispered Duncan.

"It beats me," I said. "Maybe this is the cellar." The car was as dark as your alimentary canal. There was nothing to show that anyone had ever been there—in fact, I realized suddenly, there wasn't even the racket of their clashing air-conditioning pumps.

"Spooky," I whispered. "Let's go someplace else."

Well, it was the wrong thing to do, on the face of it. The darker and the deserteder, the better a place was for our purposes. But there was something so lonesome and desolate about that corridor that we didn't stop to think things over. We piled back into the car and turned to Cleelock, and Cleelock turned to the board of buttons. He reached up for the handiest one. The door slid closed, and we braced ourselves to see what floor we'd land on this time. The door opened.

Sunlight poured in.

"Holy heaven!" gasped Cleelock. "We're back on the roof!"

One glance convinced me—it was a roof, all right. "Don't just stand there," I begged. "Get us out of here before the pinkies realize we're back!"

Cleelock nodded quickly and stretched out his hand. Just as his finger was settling on a button Duncan stopped him with a quick, incredulous gesture. "Wait a minute," he said. "Take a look around. This isn't the same roof!"

That gave us to think. I gaped out onto the roof, and what Duncan said was incontrovertibly the truth.

I vividly remembered the other roof. There had been a sort of glassy-pavemented path, and well-kept trees and bushes, and the pond. And most of all, there had been the pinkies. Here there were none of those things. Here there were only a few patches of scraggly grass. And the edge of the roof was much nearer, because this roof was not very large.

Cleelock spat angrily. "Characters," he said. "They build houses with two roofs."

Duncan said wonderingly, "That other roof—could we have been mistaken? Was it just a terrace, maybe? A gallery sticking out from one of the lower floors?"

Cleelock snorted. "And the rest of the building invisible, huh? Did you see any higher stories—or do you see any now?"

"Well, no. But, Tommy—"

"But Tommy nothing! Terrace, the man says. How could it be a terrace?"

"All right, Steinmetz. What was it? *Two* roofs, like you said?"

Cleelock's truculence puffed away. "Search me," he said weakly; "all I know is, I am not happy."

I could see the other buildings about us. They were tall towers and spires, not like the cubes I remembered seeing as we approached the city. Then I had an idea. I said, "Let's settle the argument. If it was a terrace, we'll be able to see it over the side of the roof. Why not take a look?"

"Why not?" echoed Duncan. The three of us headed for the edge . . . cautiously, because the architect of this edifice had neglected to include a guard rail in his plans. We peered down, afflicted with severe vertigo.

No terrace. In fact, nothing at all. Nothing but a straight, sheer breath-taking drop that looked to be a thousand light-years, and must in fact have been at least a mile.

The three of us recoiled from that murderous brink and stood still yards away, quieting our shattered nerves. "*What* a dope," moaned Cleelock. "You still want to look for that terrace? Maybe it's on the other side."

"No," said Duncan, and there was a definite note of strain in his voice. "No, it's not on the other side."

I looked at him curiously. "How do you know?"

"Take a look." He waved weakly off into space. "Look beyond that pinkish sort of tower over to the right. Way off on the horizon—see it?"

I peered out over the edge of the room. There was a strong breeze blowing, and it made my eyes water. I had difficulty in focusing, and while I was squinting Cleelock spotted it. "You mean—oh, yeah. It's another city. Looks all cubical, like this one."

"No," said Duncan. "*Not* like this one. Do you recognize that purple thing between the city and us?"

"Why, no. That is, it does look a little familiar—ulp!"

Cleelock abruptly ran out of words, and just about that time I saw what they were talking about.

There was a cubical kind of city. Before it, made tiny by the distance but still recognizable, was a purple torpedo of a rocket ship. The very rocket in fact, in which we had come.

"But that's impossible," I said reasonably. "That's the city we're *in*."

4

We stood gaping at that city for quite a while before we could believe it; and then we weren't sure. It was a good fifteen miles from us. Fifteen miles that we had covered apparently, in the time it took for the elevator door to open and shut. But how?

Cleelock said tentatively, "That elevator must not have been an elevator, I guess."

"Then what was it?"

He shrugged. "I don't know what you'd call it. Maybe a rocket, or a subway, or something; whatever it is, it sure got us from there to here in a hurry."

Duncan said practically, "Well, let's not worry about it. The important thing is, what are we going to do? As I see it we're in a pretty bad jam, and no relief in sight. We're stuck on Ganymede. We've got nothing to eat, no weapons, no friends. The only people we know on the whole planet want to dunk us in what looks like a sulphuric-acid swimming pool."

I said, "We still have our knives; at least, I have mine. Maybe we could catch one of the pinkies, and force him to take us to the rocket, and then—"

Cleelock snorted. "And then *what*? I left my pilot's license in my other suit."

"That's right," Duncan chimed in. "We can't fly a rocket. Even if we could, there's something else. What's all this talk about *forcing* a pinky to do anything? We tried that, remember? And look what happened?"

"Well, I guess you're right," I admitted. "They don't seem to mind the idea of death. The whole thing is screwy." I pondered on the matter for a second. "Maybe it was a bluff," I suggested. "I wondered if the Boss actually thought we would kill him, back there on the other roof. Maybe he thought we were bluffing, and ran a counter-bluff of his own, and it worked."

"I think not," Duncan said meditatively. "He believed us all right. You know, Tommy, the more I think about it, the more I'm struck by something you told us."

Cleelock said, "And what was that?"

"You said the Boss claimed to be a dog. Well—maybe he is."

I said doubtfully, "We've been over this once before. You had the idea that it meant the pinkies weren't the ruling race on this planet—that they were just domestic animals of some kind. But if it isn't them, who is it? Surely we'd expect to see the ruling race of a planet. It can't be the girl—the Boss said she was just a specimen like us, and only one of her at that."

Duncan spread his hands. "I give up," he announced resignedly. "It just doesn't add up. Things check to a certain point. The pinkies think of themselves as pets; they are willing to be killed in order to do their jobs—they even offer themselves as *food* for us. But right there the proposition collapses. If they don't run this planet, who does?"

"The redhead's pet monster, maybe," Cleelock suggested, and we all laughed grimly.

Duncan stared around us. He said, "We haven't solved the main question. What do we do?"

There was a silence. Then Cleelock said, "I know one thing; we can't just let things ride—we'd starve to death. How about trying out Nick's suggestion?"

"You mean forcing one of the pinkies to take us to the ship?" I asked.

"No. Not one of the pinkies—the girl." He ran an irate hand through his hair. "I don't care what the Boss says—if his race doesn't rule this planet, the girl's must. He can't pass her off as human. You know what she looked like. Pretty, yes. Human—good Lord, no—not with that hair. But believe me—human or not, there never was a woman that I couldn't order around. Let me handle her—that's all I ask."

Duncan looked at me doubtfully. I said, "What can we lose?"

"All right." He nodded, and turned back to the—well, let's keep calling it an elevator.

The door of the car was closed.

Cleelock tore his hair. "Wouldn't you know it?" he moaned. "Say! Does that mean somebody's using the thing—somebody that might be chasing us with it?"

"Probably," Duncan said in a flat tone. And the expression of despair on his face added the words: *And if so, what can we do about it?*

Cleelock closed his eyes. "Well," he said, and his voice was like a prayer, "there must be some way to open that door. We'd better find it. And when we do, the plan still goes."

But it didn't go, really, because we couldn't open the door.

We hunted high and low on the blank face of it, and found—nothing. Not even a design. Nothing that looked like a button, or a lever, or a switch, or anything else that might help us to get out of there. The plan was a complete flop before it got started.

We gave up, finally, and scouted the rest of the roof. There, too, we drew a complete blank. There was nothing that could help us. The roof was a plain, featureless rectangle, with the boxlike "elevator" cage in the center, grassy turf covering its whole surface and the sheer, frightening drop of a mile on all sides.

Cleelock lying on his belly while Duncan and I sat on his heels reported that he could see no windows over the edge. And, even if he had, we scarcely could have reached them. We had no ladder. The grass could not well have been plaited into a rope, though we thought of it—it was about the consistency of boiled asparagus. I suppose we could have tied our belts together—but what could we have moored them to?

No, there was no way of getting off that roof. And there was also nothing to eat.

We sat in front of the sealed door and waited for something to happen. Duncan said speculatively, "I bet they find us pretty quick. There were only about two hundred buttons in the car. Trial and error will do it."

Hopefully, I put in, "Well, maybe not. Most of the other floors—or whatever you call them—must offer a little more concealment than this one. They'll have to investigate every possible hiding place, and that might take quite a while."

Duncan said tiredly, "All that means is that we have a chance of starving to death. The hell with it. We're not going anywhere—let's not kid ourselves."

We thought that over for a while in silence. I squinted up at the lavender sky and saw that the sun—small at this distance, but bright—was rapidly approaching the horizon. By the conditioning of long habit, I began to feel sleepy.

"We ought to post a guard and turn in," I suggested.

Cleelock nodded drowsily and Duncan, who was still wide-awake, said, "All right. I'll take the first turn. You can go to sleep any time you like. But"—his eyes went to the edge of the roof, not twenty feet away—"try not to roll out of bed!"

Duncan was nudging me, and I woke up. It was night, but there were more stars out than I had ever seen. Duncan's face was clearly visible in their light.

I yawned. "Did anything exciting happen?"

He shook his head. "Not a blame thing. Oh, there's something funny way off on the horizon. But it's not very exciting. Just a lot of reddish light—looks like a big fire, maybe."

I stood up and looked where he was pointing. The sky was discolored with savage red, silhouetting the elevator cage. But it was a long way off indeed. "Too far away to bother us," I said. "Okay, you can go to sleep; I'm awake now."

He lay down and I began walking around, wishing I had a cigarette.

It was becoming very cold indeed on the roof, and I was grateful for my leather flight jacket. I looked around me with some interest. Even though we were in the "We who are about to die—" category, it was still a unique situation, and I was curious about our surroundings.

Overhead, I saw, were the familiar constellations. I picked out the Dipper and the wobbly W of Cassiopeia, unchanged by a mere hundred-million-mile shift in parallax. They did seem oddly bright, though nothing else about them was strange. I could see easily the components of the binary in the cup of the dipper, and Arcturus, to the south, was almost too brilliant to look at. The thin atmosphere, I thought.

In the monochromatic starlight the blue of the grass faded out, and the gaily colored towers that were all around us had bleached to a uniform gray. There was not a light in them. No windows, of course; I remembered that there had been no windows. But still, I would have expected some kind of light in a city, even if it were only reflected up from the ground below.

Greatly daring, I crawled on my hands and knees to the edge of the roof and looked down.

I am a phlegmatic type, I think; surely not one of those who suffer from desires to fling themselves off high places. But, looking down into that yawning ebony chasm in that deserted city, I felt the lure of it calling to

me. It was so utterly, entirely black. Even the outlines of
the adjacent structures faded into an inky pool. So
black that it seemed a sort of midnight well, and I had
the feeling that I could leap off into that thick, clinging
vacuum and swim about in it.

But, fortunately, I didn't try it; I scuttled backward
from the edge of the roof and stood up.

Utter blackness. It seemed we were in a ghost city.
Not a sound, not a glimmer of light.

I had a sudden idea, and peered out toward where I
had seen the cube city. It was still there and, sure
enough, as I had expected it shone! There was life in
that city, beyond doubt. There were no yellowish dots
of luminescence such as you see in an Earthly skyline,
no windows or lighted advertising signs. But a bluish
glow pervaded it, outlining its boxlike buildings clearly
enough even at fifteen miles' distance.

I had kept my watch running. The time it indicated,
set to a time zone on a planet hundreds of millions of
miles away, meant nothing at all, but at least it could be
used to give me an idea of the passing hours. Two hours
of solitary vigil, I decided, would be plenty. Then I
would let Cleelock take over.

I leaned against the "elevator" box and allowed
myself to drift off into reverie. It was a pleasant feeling
. . . until I caught myself just as I was falling forward
onto my face, and knew I had almost been asleep. I
roused myself and began walking around again.

The reddish glow was still silhouetting the box, but
far brighter than before. Intrigued, I walked around the
box.

A glowing semicircle of light burst upon me. The size
of a hundred moons, blotched and streaked with red
and purplish light.

It was Jupiter!

I stared at it in reverent fascination. A fantastic sight,
even by the fantastic standards of the fantastic place we
were in. I saw the cloudy areas of its supposed con-

tinents and seas far more clearly than I remembered
seeing them in the imaginative drawings I had cherished
in my youth. So near and so huge—I almost imagined
that I could reach out and thrust my fist through it.

"Jupiter," I whispered; "that cinches it." And at
once the strangeness of our predicament reached me as
it never had before. We were on Ganymede, all right . . .
and a long, long way from home.

I kept my eyes on the tremendous disk, in absorption.
By the time the two hours were up the roof was
illuminated almost as brightly as by day, with the vast
Jovian circle staring down at us over the top of the
elevator. Cleelock was stirring restlessly in the light, and
I had no compunctions about waking him.

He stared round-eyed at the planet overhead. "What
the devil!" he gasped.

I told him what it was and he nodded, wide-awake.
Our voices woke Duncan and the three of us talked excitedly about the magnificent sight, until Duncan's
practical mind took us onto a more urgent subject.

"Damn, but I'm hungry," he said ruefully.

That put the quietus on any further talk about ab-
stractions. We were all hungry, and there seemed to be
nothing we could do about it. Cleelock ordered,
"Forget it. Go back to sleep."

It seemed to be the best advice possible under the cir-
cumstances and Duncan and I tried to put it into effect.
But we didn't succeed. Because just as we lay down and
closed our eyes we heard a surprised yelp from Cleelock
and the metallic sound of a door sliding open.

We leaped to our feet. The door to the "elevator"
box had opened. And out of it stepped our gorgeous,
feather-haired traveling companion and her two-legged
pet!

"Grab her, Tommy!" I yelled, and Cleelock jumped
to do it. The girl's hand went to her mouth in shock and
bewilderment, but she put up no resistance at all. After
the initial surprise she merely stared at him with

resigned loathing. Looking somewhat foolish, he released her arms after a moment and just stood there in an attitude of threat.

Duncan and I closed in on her, me waving my silly little knife. "Perfect!" Cleelock exulted. "We couldn't ask for anything more! The very person we want, and she comes walking into our arms!"

"What'll we do with her?" I asked.

Cleelock hesitated. "Well—make her take us to the ship."

"And how are we going to get that across to her?"

"I'll try," Duncan volunteered. He fixed the girl with his third-degree stare. "Do you speak English?" he demanded.

She looked at him in wondering silence.

"I said, do you speak English?" he repeated. *"Parlez-vous francais? Panymayoo parusski? Parlate italiano? Sprechen sie Deutsch? Se habla—I mean, habla Espanol?"*

She frowned uncertainly, then essayed a peal of music.

Cleelock said, "Look, linguist, quit wasting time. Suppose she did speak one of those languages. What good would it do us? *We* don't."

Duncan shrugged uncomfortably. "Let me try again," he begged. He snapped his fingers to focus her attention, then made an effort at sign language. He pointed to the elevator door, then down, then to us, then up into the sky with a broad, sweeping motion. The girl gaped at him in bewilderment.

"You're doing fine," Cleelock said in disgust. "How do you expect her to figure that one out? I *know* what you're driving at, and even so those handies of yours confuse me." He scratched his head thoughtfully. "This palaver isn't getting us anywhere at all," he said. "Let's try direct action."

"Sure," Duncan said. "How?"

"We'll drag her into the elevator. Maybe she'll get the idea. If she doesn't, all right—we'll just keep pushing buttons till we get to where we want to go. And let's step on it—before somebody else decides to use the car again.''

"Okay," I said—it was as good an idea as any. "What about the dog?"

"We'll leave that here," said Cleelock, the masterful. "Let me show you how."

He attracted the girl's attention and pointed to the collar around her neck, gesturing her to take it off. She gazed wide-eyed, uncomprehending. He touched the dog-like beast, pointed to its collar, ran his finger along the leash to her own, repeated the take-off gesture.

Then she got it. She stumbled back in sheer horror. I cannot think of any obscene or menacing gesture he could have made that would have sparked a more horrified response in an Earthgirl. The redhead's eyes were wide with fright and revulsion.

"Oh, Lord," groaned Cleelock. "Now what's the matter?" Impulsively, he grabbed the leash and yanked at it.

That did it. She shrieked in terror—which, incidentally, tore my heart out with compassion—and her hands flew helplessly to her throat. There was a *click* and the collar came off in her hands. She set it gently down on the ground, touched the beast in farewell, and waited for the worst.

"You see" bragged Cleelock, grinning broadly. "Now we can get going! Come on, you"— he prodded the girl toward the cab—"let's make haste while Jupiter shines!"

She went without resistance, and the three of us followed close behind. When we were inside she looked up and saw the beast had been deserted, gazing after us with dimmed, mindless eyes. As she watched it looked away and, like a grazing sheep, began drifting over toward the edge of the building. Then she went wild.

"Hold onto her, Nick!" Cleelock yelled. "Don't let her out."

I had her—but she was a terrific, squirming handful.

"She's afraid her pal will fall off the roof," I panted.

"Never mind that," Cleelock ordered. "We can't worry about him. Hang on." He stared at the array of buttons, reached up and touched one.

Just as his finger came to rest on it the girl gave a squawk like a steam calliope and broke loose; she lunged out of the door.

"Hey!" I yelled, and jumped after her. I brought her down with a flying tackle, but she wriggled free like a greased dolphin and chased after the animal, now perilously close to the unfenced edge of the roof.

I saw that she caught it and led it to safety. But it didn't matter particularly to me at that time.

Because, glancing over my shoulder, I also saw that the door to the elevator-thing had closed once more. And my friends, no doubt, were back in the other city, feeling as foolish, and lost, and worried as I was myself.

5

The redhead came ambling back to me, smiling happily, the silver collar of the dog's leash pressed lovingly to her throat. She didn't appear to resent the rough handling I'd given her at all.

I got up and brushed at the bluish grass stains on my legs. Candidly, I was worried. It had been bad enough with Cleelock and Duncan to share my misery, but with them gone off to heaven-knows-where it was far worse. Still . . . this was a remarkably pretty girl, I told myself, and the situation did have some attractive angles. In the ruby light from Jupiter, overhead the flaming crimson of her hair washed out, and she might have been an exceptionally fine-haired Terrestrial blonde.

She grinned at me in a friendly fashion and sang a questioning phrase.

"It beats me, honey," I told her. "Try singing it as a polka."

She looked at me blankly. I pointed to the closed door. "Open," I ordered, without much hope.

Another peal of music.

"I said *open*," I repeated. I remembered the knife

46

and held it before me, pointed at her as menacingly as I
could manage. "Open that door!"

No music this time. Instead, she laughed at me with
broad good humor. When she was quite through
laughing she reached out and plucked the knife from my
incredulous fingers. She stared at it for a second, then
negligently tossed it up and away. It sailed through the
air, and dropped out of sight into the chasm beyond the
edge of the roof. She watched it gravely, then turned
and gave me another homefolks smile.

"Well, I looked good on that one, I must say," I said
bitterly. "All right, pal. Now what shall we do?"

She patted my shoulder comfortingly. Then she
handed me the silver collar.

I stood, holding it in my hand. It tingled oddly,
almost as though charged with a minute electric current.
I started to hand it back to her, a little nervously, but
she halted me. She gestured the act of holding the thing
to my throat, as she herself had been doing before.

"Huh?" I said.

A peal of peremptory music. She frowned and repeated the gesture.

"Oh, lady," I said, "I haven't got time for games.
I've got a lot of worrying to catch up on." I handed the
collar back to her and walked over to the closed door of
the *soidisant* elevator. I was running my hands over it
for the twentieth hopeless time when she tapped me on
the shoulder.

I turned. She was holding the collar out to me again, a
beseeching, lost look in her eyes.

I began to lose my patience. "Good Lord," I said in
exasperation. "Leave me alone." I walked away to stare
off into the red-lit night at the distant city of cubes.

The black chasm, now shot through with a dull,
mean-looking red, was below me. I looked into it—
from a safe distance—with a sort of grim enjoyment. At
least, I thought, I could always jump . . .

A gentle peal of music from behind me. I leaped a
foot—away from the edge of the building.

She was holding the collar out to me again. I thought

of a line from my high-school Shakespeare. Something about, "thrice offering a kingly crown, which he did thrice refuse."

"Honey, *don't* sneak up behind me like that," I said.

She smiled forgivingly. Then, still smiling, she walked toward me, her arms outstretched to me. It was a strange time for romance, I thought . . .

But she stepped up close to me, until her small, pointed chin was only an inch from my breastbone. Her arms went about my neck. It took me a split fraction of a second to make up my mind what she was after, and that was entirely too much time.

My subconscious woke up and began squawking, *Danger!* But it was too late. I felt something chill and metallic circle my neck. There was an instant of numbing electrical shock; I heard the *click* as she fastened the catch . . .

And the collar was locked about my neck.

Someone was speaking to me, not in words.

It was not a voice, but I understood it. It was not my own thoughts, but it was in my brain.

It was a thought, an emotion, and a mood. It was three things—or more than three things—expressed at once, yet each standing alone. There was a command of non-fear; a broad soundless laughter; a memory of my amusing obstinacy.

In English, it might have been said like this: *Do not be afraid, Earthman. You struggled very hard, but— laughter—the struggle is over.*

I stared incredulously at the girl. She was watching me with amusement on her delicately shaped face, but surely it was not her thoughts that were invading my mind. "Who—who are you?" I said aloud.

Again that echoing laughter. Then suddenly a picture was in my mind, so vivid that it blotted out what my eyes were seeing and replaced the view with a vision of . . . of the pallid, deformed, dog-like thing to which I was leashed, in all its idiot hideousness!

I said feebly, "No. Oh, no!"

That is what I am, said the soundless voice in my brain, with sadness and humorous resignation woven into the meaning of the thought. *That is what my people have been for a million years*.

What happened then is an inglorious episode in my career, and I had rather not dwell on it. I was panic-stricken. Things were just suddenly too much for me . . . and I rebelled.

I clawed at the collar around my neck, fumbling for a catch that I couldn't find. I'm not sure, but I think that I must have been screaming. My fright awoke a responsive alarm in the mind that was within my mind, and I sensed that, for an infinitesimal second, it drew away in doubt.

Then . . . it returned, warm, strong, reassuring. *Sleep, Earthman*, said the voice in my mind with gentle solicitude. *Sleep—*

I slept.

There were chaotic dreams of things beyond my understanding, and a feeling of receiving instruction from a master. Then I was awake.

It wasn't a real sleep, I suppose. I don't think it could have lasted more than a moment, because when I opened my eyes there was no waking-up drowsiness, and I saw that the girl was standing just as she had stood before, watching me expectantly.

"Is it over?" she asked.

I nodded, and started to reply, "Yes." But I did a rapid doubletake which left me goggling at her. Her voice had been the peal of music—yet I had understood what she said:

She saw my confusion and, understanding, laughed. "I see that it is over," she said in that strange music, answering her own question. "How do you feel? Can you understand me?"

I nodded speechlessly.

"Then tell me how you feel," she demanded. "If you can understand, you can talk."

Well, that made sense, of course. But nevertheless, it

was absurd. I tried, unbelievingly, to speak. And, though I could not have said how it happened, a musical phrase came to my mind, and I uttered it, and knew that it meant: "I feel fine!"

But it was a lie. I was dizzy, and bewildered beyond endurance.

I sat limply on the sparse blue grass. The movement tugged the leash about my neck, and the dog-beast—the thing that just had been inside my mind—croaked protestingly, then slid to its knees with a jolt and stared brainlessly around.

The girl said, "Here—let me take the collar off. He has withdrawn rapport. It is so difficult, the first time. It tires him, and it is bad for you."

I let her lean, strong fingers touch something in the collar. It fell into jointed halves, and she held it in her hand. She was smiling at me.

"Tell me what this is all about," I begged her.

She hesitated, and then she began to tell me.

I was in a plastic, credulous mood, and if what she said had been obvious fabrication I would have believed it anyway, for lack of the will to doubt. But it was clearly, fantastically the truth.

"First," she said, "you are in no danger. There was some danger but it has passed. There was the danger that your mind would not survive the contact with the mind of the Khreen."

"Khreen?" It was a warbling, ascending musical note, the same word the Boss had used back in the rocket. I waved at the drowsing beast. "Do you mean *that*?"

"Yes," she said. She looked at the animal, and in her look I saw both tenderness and genuine respect. Respect for that hunk of low-grade beast!

"Explain this to me," I begged.

She touched the beast fondly. "A million years ago," she said, "Ganymede was a civilized world. Its people were humanoid—more like myself, I think, than like you. And they were advanced in science, as you can see." She hesitated, then went on, and by and by I began to understand. There was a reason why that hulk of an animal could command respect and affection from as brilliant a girl as she. For it was a beast, all right . . . but it was also the finest mind the universe had ever spawned!

"Perhaps," she said, "their science was too far advanced. They knew ways of changing the stuff of life itself—radiations, surgical techniques, things I cannot understand. And through that came their great catastrophe."

The Khreen, as I learned to call them, had grown and matured, covering their own planet with their works and sending scouts to every planet of the system. But they had found—nothing. Half the worlds were bleak ice; some were roaring inferno. Two—Earth and Venus— showed life, but nothing that could be called intelligence.

Thwarted in the search for another race's companionship, they returned to their own world, determined to create an intelligent race! One by one they examined and tested the life-forms of their planet, and one by one they were discarded. Until they came to a small-brained amphibian, rust-colored and few in numbers, that lived in their swamps. It was the thing they sought, far enough along the road of evolution to be of value, and yet it had not specialized.

They took that little rust-colored reptile from the swamps and put it in their laboratories. They charted a path for its evolution to follow, and started it on the way with their miraculous rays.

Then, something went wrong.

"It seemed to be a self-sustaining reaction," the girl said slowly. "I—I'm not sure exactly what happened, because the knowledge of it was lost in the upheaval that followed, and I probably could not understand anyhow. But the rays went wild. And all over Ganymede, evolution was uncontrolled."

I took in the meaning of her words slowly. It was a horrible vision that they conjured up. As she spoke, I imagined free mutation of species, monsters being born.

It had not lasted long, she told me, but in the brief time that the rays were loose in the world, it destroyed their status quo. In effect, a sentence of execution had been passed on every person and every beast that was alive on Ganymede, and it was only a matter of waiting until the corpses cooled. For slow, horrible radiation burns destroyed them.

Within a year the only living things were the new-born . . . and they were monstrous.

"Every species threw off mutants," she said. "Uncounted hundreds of thousands of them. Some had many heads, or no limbs at all; some had rubbery skeletons, some were born insane, lived insane, died insane. Some were sterile, and they died. Some were just never meant to live . . . and they died. Of all the thousands of new types that the rays spawned, only two found mates, and bred true, and survived. One was the Khreen—" she patted the dog-beast. "The other was what you call the pinkies—the descendants of the little red reptile that started the whole thing."

I shook my head wonderingly. Then, as I remembered something, I said, "The Boss was telling me something like this once. He started to tell about a race that was in solitary confinement for a million years. I didn't understand at the time, and I don't now. Is this what he was talking about?"

She nodded. "That was the horror of the whole thing," she said seriously. "For the Khreen came to look like animals, but they were not animals. They survived the rays—but their tragedy was almost worse than if they had become extinct."

I stared incredulously at the dog-beast. "You say this isn't an animal? Well, it would have fooled me. Did—did the rays work in reverse, maybe—making it an atavism or something?"

"No," she said. "The rays did their work, only too well. The Khreen evolved far beyond humanity. What you see before you is superman."

I laughed tentatively. "Sure," I said, going along with the gag. "I can tell that just by looking."

"Really," she said, and I saw that she was not joking. "The Khreen evolved, but in an unfortunate direction. The brain of the Khreen became a marvelous instrument for pure thought. The body—evolved too. You know that, even in your own body and mine, some of the work of directing your actions is done by what you call reflexes?"

"Yes."

"And that these reflexes are not in the brain, but in a group of nerves in your spinal column?"

"I'd heard that," I admitted.

She nodded decisively. "Well, in the evolved body of the Khreen, the work of that group of motor-nerves was increased sharply. In fact—it took over every physical function. The nerves which led to the brain itself atrophied and disappeared. The body became independent, with its own tiny 'brain,' a separate nerve system, complete control of its musculature. The brain and the body became separate individuals . . . and the result was a godlike mind, in the body of a beast!"

"Good Lord," I said.

I lay back, staring up at the round face of Jupiter overhead, thinking it over. Questions flooded into my brain—too many for me to ask even one, because each question was driven out by a dozen new ones before I could get it to my lips. I felt benumbed and bewildered . . . and a physical thing, forcing itself to my consciousness, was demanding more and more attention. I was hungry.

I stood up, and I felt faint. Small wonder—since the pinkies had awakened us in the space ship, I had had but two meals!

The girl saw me reeling. "What is the matter?" she asked in musical alarm.

"Nothing much," I said apologetically. "I'm just hungry."

"Hungry? Oh." She frowned at me in concentration. "We—we don't eat, here," she said finally. "Still, I suppose—"

"Don't eat?" I yelped. "How do you survive?"

"Why, we use the life-waters," she said, surprised. "Your food does nothing but supply you with energy and materials to replace wastage. The life-waters do the same thing. Only much more simply—by absorption through the skin—and without the contamination in ordinary food. Also, they have a germicidal effect," she added delicately. "I understand your system is flooded with germs."

"Life-waters," I said, rolling the sound of it on my tongue. "Well, all right. Where do we go to find these life-waters?"

"On the roof of the Entrance Building, for one place." She gestured back to the cubical city. "Where you and your friends got so—ah—excited."

"Let's go," I said, "I'm game."

She waved her hand before the blank face of the "elevator" door—only she told me, when I asked her, that it was not an elevator but a matter transmitter. The door opened. No buttons, no nothing . . . it was some sort of electronic capacitance control, I suppose. Inside, with me and the Khreen crowding after her, she pressed a button and the door closed, opened, and we were back on the other roof again.

"Very clever piece of equipment," I said, staggering slightly in dizziness. Then, remembering, "By the way, you haven't told me how I learned to speak your language."

"The Khreen taught you, of course. Telepathically, while you were wearing the collar. That's all the collar is—a telepathy-wave amplifier, and the wire is a conducting cable."

I started to ask more questions, but, "Later," she said firmly. "First get in the pool."

I looked around with a slight, involuntary shiver. There was no one else on the roof, just the two of us—and the Khreen. The pool, there before me, was just as I remembered it . . . limpid orange flame.

"Go ahead," she said. "It won't hurt you."

I hesitated. "All right. Shall I dive in with my clothes on?"

"Of course not! Take them off."

"Then turn your back," I said. "On that I insist."

The shrug of her shoulders denoted complete lack of comprehension, but, after giving me a wondering gaze, she complied. "How long must I stand like this?" she asked plaintively.

"I'll tell you when to turn around," I said . . .

It took me several seconds to get up my nerve, but finally I jumped.

The liquid was warm . . . that was my first impression. Other than that, it felt like nothing at all, except plain water. I was a little disappointed.

It was curiously soothing, though. I lay back in it, relaxed and floating, and new strength seeped back into me. I felt warm, sheltered, comfortable. Almost I could have drifted off to sleep . . .

"Can I turn around yet?" the girl demanded.

I blinked and splashed myself to a standing position. "Nope! But tell me, how long to stay in this?"

She said, "As long as you like. You've been in it long enough for about three days, though—you might as well come out."

Obediently I crawled out, scraped the golden, fiery drops off me with the flat of my hand, climbed back into my clothing. I felt like a new man.

I looked at her with revived appreciation. "Say," I asked, "have you got a name?"

"A name?" Puzzlement in the musical voice. "No."

"Then I'll give you one," I decided. "I think I'll call you—Honey."

She repeated the English word. Her attempts were amusing, but I had another question on my mind and couldn't take time to laugh at her.

"You forgot to tell me your own story," I reminded her. "What about it?"

*   *   *

She turned around and looked at me. She said, "I don't know my story. Only what the pinkies have told me. You see, I was very young when I came here."

"From Earth?"

She nodded. "The first expedition. The one that brought you back was the second. They found me and my parents, and took us here—for curiosities mostly, I think, but also to use in their laboratories."

I grimaced. "That doesn't sound very good," I observed. "You mean, to cut up?"

"Oh, no. The Khreen are still trying to control the evolutionary rays. They could do nothing with my parents, because they were mature, fully formed. On myself, they say, they had limited success." She touched her corona of pinkish, feather-light hair. "You are too old too," she added, smiling elfinly; "they were so disappointed!"

"Yeah, but what about your parents? What happened to them?"

"They died," she said sadly. "When I was very young. Oh, it was not the fault of the Khreen. They were sick when they were found, and they could not be saved."

I nodded. It checked well enough, and I was relieved to find that, after all, she at least had once been human. I *wanted* her to be human . . .

But I had one more question. "You said the Khreen were in solitary confinement, didn't you? What did you mean?"

She said, "Oh, that is over now. But for almost a million years, they neither saw, nor heard, nor felt anything. They were telepathic among themselves, and they could communicate mind to mind. But you see, on the whole planet there was no other mind at all that they could reach?"

"Not even the pinkies?"

"Not at first. After a long, long time the pinkies began to have intelligence. The rays gave them a good start, but it was not quite enough. It took almost a

million years until their brains were fully enough
developed to receive the thoughts of the Khreen. Even
today, it is not perfect. That is why they—and we—use
these." She touched the silver collar of the beast, which
was apparently asleep on the ground beside us.

"But once the pinkies had attained intelligence," she
went on, "it was simple. Contact was still very incomplete, but some of the pinkies turned out to be sen-
sitives, and the Khreen began to suggest things to their
minds. The first step"—she smiled at the thought—
"was to persuade them to domesticate the Khreen!"

"You mean, use them for something?"

"Yes. As beasts of burden. It didn't harm the minds
of the Khreen, of course—they could feel nothing. And
it kept the two races together, until the Khreen had time
to teach them something of science, and develop the
thought-collar for better control. They were helped a lot
by the fact that their cities still stood, and some of their
tools were still in them."

I looked around me. "Is this one of them?"

Her face registered faint revulsion. "No. This is what
the pinkies built for themselves. So ugly! But the other
city—where we were just now—that is one of the old
ones. Much more beautiful. I go there often."

She stopped talking, and I began to pace around,
digesting her information. It was hard to believe, but it
had to be true. Everything fitted. Nothing that would fit
the facts could be any less fantastic.

I spotted Cleelock's discarded knife where he had
thrown it, and idly picked it up. Then I had an idea.

"Say," I said, "why couldn't the Khreen use this
telepathy gadget on their own brains? Not the real
brains—the others, the ones that control the bodies?"

She shook her head. "Telepathy," she reminded me,
"can only occur between two full-fledged mature
minds. The body brains are very rudimentary, really.
They hope, perhaps some day, to evolve a little farther
. . . but they were afraid to take the chance on another
catastrophe like the one before. However, they do per-
form experiments—such as the one on me."

I was about to speak, but something halted me.
Something that was prodding at my brain—as though
someone were shouting at me, urgently, soundlessly, a
long way off.

I turned to the girl, and she had felt it too. Her eyes
went wide with self-reproach.

"The Khreen!" she gasped. "I've been out of rapport—"

She clutched at the collar of the neglected genius-
beast—still asleep, to all external appearances—beside
her. She snapped it around her neck, close to the
medulla oblongata, I realized, and began "talking" to
the alert mind within the sleeping beast. I saw an expression of surprise and alarm cross her face, and she
stared at me almost with hostility.

"What's the matter?" I asked anxiously.

She frowned in agitation. "Your friends are in
trouble!" she said. "They've managed, somehow, to
get into the rocketship. They've closed the ports—and
they're trying to take off!"

"The fools!" I groaned. "They can't possibly fly it;
they'll be killed!"

"Of course," she said soberly. "But that's not the
worst. One of the Khreen is trapped inside!"

6

We were back in the "elevator" in a fraction of a moment, all three of us. Before I had a chance to collect my thoughts the door was open again, and we were back in the corridor on the ground floor.

As before, the canoe-shaped car was waiting for us, with a pinky in it at the controls. He was working up a fit of fury, and when he saw me it exploded. "Savages! Cannibals! Murderers!" he yelled, and by the tone, even more than by the fact that he spoke in English, I knew him as the Boss.

"Quiet down," I advised him, speaking in the musical tongue so that the girl could understand. "I didn't do anything."

"Hah!" he said bitterly. "You are all alike, you specimens. Fiends!"

"Leave us not call names, Boss." I begged. "All they're trying to do is get away from here; you can't blame them for that."

"Yes I can!"

"Well, it's your own fault," I said wearily. "You

scared us half to death, you and your bad manners. What happened?''

"Bad things happened! The two fiends came out of that building over there—'' he pointed with his webbed paw. "One of us saw them, but by the time he was able to get a car to chase them, they were halfway to the ship, jumping along like anything. Great big fiends!''

"Well, let's get out there,'' I said. "Maybe I can talk sense into their heads. Though, heaven knows, you've made it a tough job.''

He snarled at me. "Get in,'' he said sourly.

We did, and he played with the board in front of him. The car zoomed ahead, swerved in a racing turn and scooted for the purple rocket.

"What's the score?'' I yelled to the girl over the noise of the wind rushing past. "Can they see us coming?''

She shook her head. "There's no way of contacting them from outside.''

"Great!'' I said in surprise and chagrin. "Then what's the sense of coming out here?''

She explained hastily, "I mean, as long as we're on the ground. There *is* one way you can attract their attention. You'll have to climb up the nose of the ship to where the piloting compartment is—the Khreen who's trapped inside thinks that that's where they are, according to the telepathic messages he sent to *my* Khreen. Once you're up there, they'll be able to see you through the nose of the ship. There's a port that will open when they release it from inside—'' She described the port to me.

I said, "Well, it sounds easy enough. What's the catch?''

She looked at me with sorrow and a trace of fear—not fear for herself, I thought exultantly, but for me. "The catch is that they are trying to get the ship started. And if they do—''

She bit her lip and didn't finish the sentence.

She didn't have to. I swallowed with some difficulty. "I see what you mean,'' I said. "If they win, I lose.''

*   *   *

The Boss brought the car to a stop that would have taken a quarter of an inch of rubber off the tires, if it had had rubber tires. We were under the looming nose of the ship.

The girl pointed, and I recognized the bulging glassy panel behind which lay the pilot chamber. There were metal hoops and projections spotted all over the hull, apparently to help maintenance crews. It wouldn't be very difficult to climb, in this light gravity.

I grabbed the first hoop and started lifting myself.

The girl spoke from behind me, her voice gentle. "Nick—" she pronounced it *Neek*. "Wait a moment, Neek."

I turned and let myself down again. She was out of the car, standing close with an expectant look on her face, arms half stretched out to me. She appeared exactly like a girl who wanted to be kissed. I kissed her. The appearance was not deceiving.

"Neek," she whispered, "please don't get hurt. Please."

I said, with a sort of speech impediment that I'd just picked up, "I'll try. Hey—where are you going?" She had released me, was getting back in the car.

"I must get out of blast range," she said sorrowfully, pointing at the beast in the car. "I can't endanger the Khreen. But please be safe, Neek."

I didn't waste time looking after her, but I kept an ear cocked to the dwindling sounds of the car as I began the twenty-foot climb.

It couldn't have taken more than a minute, but it was one of the very longest minutes of my life. I was expecting the worst. Vivid pictures flashed through my mind of what I would look like if Cleelock and Duncan got the rockets working before I could stop them. There were several possibilities, and I didn't like any of them. The blast of the rockets might get me, in which case I'd be a charred cinder; or if I managed to hold on until the ship attained some altitude and then fell, I'd be a battered pulp. The very best I could hope for, I decided, would be to hang on until they reached outer space . . .

in which case I would become a bloated icicle.

But by the time I had reviewed the chances, I had made it. I was clinging to the edge of the transparent cone at the nose of the ship.

Through the crystal I could see Duncan and Cleelock, furiously, working over the gadgets on the ship's control panel. By the expressions of exasperation and anxiety on their faces, they were exhorting each other to greater speed.

I banged on the window with all my strength. Nothing happened. I might as well have been sledging a bank vault with a marshmallow hammer, for all the noise I made. I yelled, but that was hopeless—they obviously couldn't hear me, because I couldn't hear them. Then I had a brilliant stroke of memory.

Cleelock's knife, which I had picked up on the roof, was still in my pocket. I took it out and hefted it. It was small, but it was made of a heavy metal, and would do the trick. I swung it against the glass.

It wasn't glass, or it would have broken. It didn't break; it gave out a low, bell-like tone, and wasn't even scratched. But inside, they heard it.

They gaped at me as if I'd been an orange-eyed monster with black wings. But finally I got it through their thick skulls that I wanted in, and how they were to accomplish same.

I tumbled inside, breathing hard in relief. "Where'd you come from?" Duncan demanded suspiciously.

"Climbed up the outside," I explained. "Listen, I've been talking to the Khreen—"

Cleelock cut in, "Never mind that! Do you know how to run one of these things?"

"No, of course not," I said. "But it doesn't matter. I tell you, I've been talking to the Khreen; you haven't got a thing to worry about. They look like beasts, I admit, but actually they're intelligent, and cultured, and—"

Cleelock's jaw was hanging as he stared at me in mixed incredulity and alarm. "Have you gone off your rocker?'' he demanded. "Are you talking about those Ganymedan hairlesses?''

"Sure. I know they don't look like much, but they mean well. They've got two brains, see? And the good brain is terrific, only it doesn't have anything to do with the body.''

Duncan said positively, "He's cracked under the strain. Should we tie him up, or something?''

Cleelock shook his head, keeping his eyes on me warily. "He's just excited," he said charitably. "Come on, let's get on with this thing; I want to go home.''

They pushed me aside and returned to the instrument board. "Try those," Cleelock suggested, pointing to a bank of red studs on the right. Duncan began jabbing them at random, in a close approach to panic.

"Hold on, fellow," I said. They snarled over their shoulders at me.

"Well," I said, "if you want to be unreasonable." I hefted the butt of the knife in my hand. With my fist closed over it, its mass converted my hand into an effective blackjack.

I selected the proper, non-lethal spot at the back of their skulls. "This hurts me more than it does you," I murmured to their backs, raising my hand for the knock-out tap . . .

Well, that was all some time ago. We've been on Ganymede pretty near a year now, and heaven only knows how long the trip out from Earth took—about a year, anyway. The Boss told me once, but he expressed it as a fraction of Jupiter's year, and we all scratched our heads for about an hour trying to remember how long Jupiter's year was. Then we gave up.

We were all lolling around the life-water pool, one morning after *carna* but just before the time to *brust*, and Duncan said, "No matter how you figure it, we've been away close on to two years. I'm beginning to feel a little homesick.''

We nodded. "I wonder how the Dodgers are making

out," Tommy said. "And the cold war—how do you suppose that's doing?"

"Yeah," Duncan said wistfully, kicking his feet into the pool and spraying orange sparks about. "It would be nice to go back."

I said, "It sure would. For one thing, I'd like to do something about—well, about legalizing—that is, I mean—" I trailed off, pointing to Honey, who was staring dreamily at the lavender sky. Cleelock and Duncan nodded, understanding perfectly. Cleelock said:

"I had a girl myself back in Memphis. Hope she's still there." He looked wistful for a moment. "In fact," he said, "I hope *Memphis* is still there."

Honey took her eyes off the sky and tossed back her gorgeous hair. In sing-song she said, "The Boss is going back to Earth on another sampling expedition soon. If you ask him, he'll probably bring a couple of extra girls for you."

"Ah!" said Tommy. Then, in English, "Maybe he could do better than that. Maybe he could bring us back to Earth."

Duncan nodded. "Back to Earth. That's where we belong, men. Back to San Diego, and that lovely fog that hangs over it all winter long. Back to Klotchweiler's store, and my old job behind the counter."

"Back," I said, "to work. To getting up when the alarm goes off and fighting my way onto the Sea Beach Express. Back to sinus trouble and the atomic bomb. And hash-house food. And insomnia and water shortages."

"And coal strikes and steel strikes," Tommy supplied, "and phone strikes and train strikes and—"

"And income tax," said Duncan. "Don't forget the income tax. Don't *ever* forget the income tax."

Tommy stood up and shook his head like a man coming out of a dream. "Leave this planet and go back to Earth," he breathed, and looked at us wide-eyed. "Fellows, who are we *kidding*?"

A generation ago, when writers got together, one of the topics that always came up was "slant." It wasn't the top priority. The two chief subjects were money and the madness of editors, and that at least has not changed. But slanting—i.e., so tailoring your work as to push an editor's buttons and make him emit a check—always finished a strong third. Slanting was one of the skills every writer tried to learn, like erasing coffee stains from a rejected story and stalling creditors until a check came in. RED MOON OF DANGER was slanted, as hard and as accurately as I could manage, to a woman named Kathleen Rafferty.

Rafferty was the editor of a general-adventure pulp called FIVE NOVELS. She had never published any science fiction. But she did publish mysteries, and what's more she paid a lot more than the existing sf pulps did; so I tried her with a detective story of mine. It didn't interest her. She had her regulars for that part of the magazine; but what she didn't have, she told me, was anybody to write science fiction, and would I like to try?

Would I? I went home and wrote with blinding

*speed—AFTER reading all the back copies of FIVE
NOVELS I could get to learn her "slant", and to try to
extrapolate it to decide what sort of sf she would publish
if she had ever published any. FIVE NOVELS was for a
general audience. Obviously (I thought) nothing too
complicated would do. It needed to be "bridge" science
fiction, and very heavily accented on the adventure and
action side; and what came out was RED MOON OF
DANGER. Rafferty received it gracefully, read it with
courteous promptness . . . and then, settling a pillow by
her head, told me that that was not it, at all. And it was
right around then that I began to question, among other
bits of consensual pulp wisdom, whether "slanting"
was ever the right thing to do.*

*It now seems pretty clear to me that it was not. The
only thing a writer has to sell is his own personal,
idiosyncratic view of the universe. If he buries that under what he believes to be an editor's eccentricities he
might as well not write at all. Kathleen Rafferty was
(and still is) an agreeable and talented person. She did
buy one or two other pieces from me, and I'm grateful
to her for her work and counsel. I'm even grateful to
her, sort of, because she did NOT buy RED MOON OF
DANGER. Bob Lowndes did, and brought me back
home where I belonged.*

Red Moon of Danger

1

Steve Templin came out of the airlock into Hadley Dome and looked around for someone to blow off steam on. Templin was fighting mad—had been that way for three days now, ever since he was ordered to report for this mysterious mission on the Moon.

Templin stripped off his pressure suit and almost threw it at the attendant. "I'm looking for Ellen Bishop," he growled. "Where can I find her?"

The attendant said deferentially, "Miss Bishop's suite is on Level Nine, sir. Just below the solarium."

"Okay," groused Templin, walking off.

"Just a second, sir," the attendant called after him. "You forgot your check. And who shall I say is calling, please?"

Templin took the metal tag and jammed it in the pocket of his tunic. "Say nothing," he advised over his shoulder. "I'm going to surprise her."

He stared contemptuously around the ornate lobby of Hadley Dome, then, ignoring the waiting elevator, headed for the wide basalt stairway that led upstairs.

With the force of gravity here on the Moon only about
one sixth as powerful as on the surface of the Earth, an
elevator was a particularly useless and irritating luxury.
It was fit, Templin thought only for the kind of washed-
out aristocrats who could afford to chase thrills for the
five hundred dollars a day it cost them to live in Hadley
Dome. Templin, a heavyweight on his home planet,
weighed little over thirty-five pounds on the Moon. He
bounded up the stairs in great soaring leaps, eight or ten
steps at a time.

On the ninth level he paused, not even winded, and
scowled about him. All over were the costly trappings of
vast wealth. To Templin's space-hardened mind, Hadley Dome was a festering sore-spot on the face of the
Moon. He glowered at the deep-piled Oriental carpet on
the floor, the lavish murals that had been painted on the
spot by the world's highest-priced artists.

Someone was coming down the long hall. Templin
turned and saw a dark, solidly-built man coming toward
him in the peculiar slow-motion walk that went with the
Moon's light gravity. Templin stopped him with a
gesture.

"I'm looking for Ellen Bishop," Templin repeated
wearily. "Where's her room?"

The dark man stopped and looked Templin over in
leisurely fashion. Judging by the gem-studded belt
buckler that adorned his brilliantly colored shorts, he
was one of the Dome's paying guests . . . which meant
that he was a millionaire at the least. He said in a cold,
confident voice: "Who the devil are you?"

Templin clamped his jaw down on his temper.
Carefully he said, "My name is Templin. Steve
Templin. If you know where Ellen Bishop's room is, tell
me; otherwise skip it."

The dark man said thoughtfully, "Templin. I know
that name—oh, yes. You're that crazy explorer, aren't
you? The one who's always hopping off to Mercury or
Venus or some other planet."

"That's right," said Templin. "Now look, for the last time—"

"What do you want to see Ellen Bishop about?" the dark man interrupted him.

Templin lost control. "Forget it," he flared. He started to walk past the dark man, but the man held out his arm and stopped him. Templin halted, standing perfectly still. "Look, mister," he said. "I've had a tough day, and you're making me mad. Take your hand off my arm."

The dark man said angrily, "By heaven, I'll have you thrown out of the Dome if you don't watch your tongue! I'm Joe Olcott!"

Templin deliberately shook the man's arm off. The dark man growled inarticulately and lunged for him.

Templin side-stepped easily. "I warned you," he said, and he brought his fist up just hard enough to make a good solid contact with the point of Olcott's jaw. Olcott grunted and, grotesquely slowly in the light gravity, he collapsed unconscious on the carpeted floor.

A gasp from behind told Templin he had an audience. He whirled; a girl in the green uniform of a maid was frozen in the doorway of one of the rooms, one hand to her mouth in an attitude of shock.

Templin saw her and relaxed, grinning. "Don't get upset about it," he told her. "He was asking for it. Now maybe *you* can tell me where Ellen Bishop's room is?"

The maid stammered, "Y-yes, sir. The corner suite, at the end of the corridor."

"Thanks."

The maid hesitated. "Did you know that that was Mr. Joseph Olcott?" she asked tentatively.

Templin nodded cheerfully. "So he told me." In a much improved frame of mind he strolled down to the door the maid had indicated. He glanced at it disapprovingly—it was carved of a single massive piece of oak, which was rare treasure on the treeless, airless moon—but shrugged and rapped it with his knuckles.

"Come in," said a girl's voice from a concealed loudspeaker beside the door, and the door itself swung open automatically. Steve walked in and discovered that he was in a well-furnished drawing room, the equal of anything on Earth.

From behind a huge desk a girl faced him. She was about twenty, hair black as the lunar night, blue eyes that would have been lovely if they had any warmth.

Templin looked around him comfortably, then took out a cigarette and put it in his lips. The chemically treated tip of it kindled to a glow as he drew in the first long puff. "I'm Steve Templin," he said. "What do you want to see me about?"

A trace of a smile curved the corners of the girl's red mouth. "Sit down, Mr. Templin," she said. "I'm glad you're here."

Templin nodded and picked out the chair closest to the desk. "I'm not," he said.

"That's hardly flattering."

Steve Templin shrugged. "It isn't intended to be. I went to work for your father because I liked him and because he gave me a free hand. After he died and you took over, I renewed my contract with the company because it was the only way I saw to keep on with my work on the Inner Planets. Now—I don't know. What do you want with me here?"

Ellen Bishop sighed. "I don't know," she confessed. "Maybe if I knew, I wouldn't have had to cancel your orders to go back to Mercury. All I know is that we need help here, and it looks like you're the only one who can provide it."

Steve asked noncommittally, "What kind of help?"

The girl hesitated. "How long have you been out of touch with what's going on?" she countered.

"You mean while I was on Mercury? About eleven months; I just got back."

Ellen nodded. "And has anyone told you about our—trouble here?"

Steve laughed. "Nobody told me anything," he said flatly. "They didn't have time, maybe. I came back

from Mercury with survey charts that took me six
months to make, showing where there are mineral
deposits that will make anything here on the Moon look
sick. All I wanted to do was turn them over to the company, pick up supplies and start out for Venus. And one
of your glorified office boys was waiting for me at Den-
ver skyport with your ethergram, ordering me to report
here. I just about had time for one real Earth meal and a
bath before I caught the rocket shuttle to the Moon.''

"Well—" the girl said doubtfully. "Suppose I begin
at the beginning, then. You know that my father
organized this company, Terralune Projects, to develop
uranium deposits here on the Moon. He raised a lot of
money, set up the corporation, made plans. He even
arranged to finance trips to other planets, like yours to
Mercury and Venus, because doing things like that
meant more to him than making money. And then he
died.''

Her face shadowed. "He died," she repeated, "and I
inherited a controlling interest in Terralune. And then
everything went to pot.''

A buzzer sounded on Ellen Bishop's desk, interrupting her. She said, "Hello," and a voice-operated
switch turned on her communicator.

A man's voice drawled, "Culver speaking. Shall I
come up now?''

Ellen hesitated. Then she said, "Yes," and flicked off
the communicator. "That's Jim Culver," she explained. "He'll be your assistant while you're here.''

"That's nice," Templin said acidly. "Assistant to do
what?''

The girl looked surprised. "Oh I didn't tell you, did
I? You're going to manage the uranium mines at
Hyginus Cleft.''

Templin opened his eyes wide and stared at her.
"Look, Bishop," he said, "I can't do that. What do I
know about uranium mines—or any other kind of
mines?''

Before the girl could answer, the door opened. A tall,

lean man drifted in, looked at Templin with mournful
eyes. "Hello," he said.

Templin nodded at him. "Get back to the question,"
he reminded the girl. "What about these mines? I'm no
miner."

The girl said, "I know you aren't. We've had three
mining engineers on the project in eight weeks. Things
are no better for them—in fact, things are worse; ask
Culver." She waved to the lean man, who was fumbling
around his pockets for a cigarette.

Culver found the cigarette and nodded confirmation.
"Trouble isn't ordinary," he said briefly. "It's things
that are—strange. Like machines breaking down. And
tunnels caving in. And pieces of equipment being
missing. Nothing that a mining engineer can handle."

"But maybe something that *you* can handle." Ellen
Bishop was looking at Templin with real pleading in her
eyes, the man from the Inner Planets thought. He said:
"Got any ideas on who's causing it? Do you think it's
just accidental? Or have you been having trouble with
some other outfit, or anything of the sort?"

Ellen Bishop bit her lip. "Not real trouble," she said.
"Of course, there's Joe Olcott . . ."

Joe Olcott. The name rang a firebell in Templin's
mind. Olcott . . . yes, of course! The chunky dark man
in the corridor—the one he had knocked out!

He grinned abruptly. "I met Mr. Olcott," he acknowledged. "Unpleasant character. But he didn't seem
like much of a menace to me."

Ellen Bishop shrugged. "Perhaps he isn't. Oh, you
hear stories about him, if you can believe them. They
say he has been mixed up in a number of things that
were on the other side of the law—that he has com-
mitted all sorts of crimes himself. But—I don't really
believe that. Only, it seems funny that we had no
trouble at all until Olcott tried to buy a controlling interest in Terralune. We turned him down—it was just a
month or so after Dad died—and from then on things
have gone from bad to worse."

Templin stubbed out his cigarette, thinking. Automatically his fingers went to his pocket, took out another, and he blew out a huge cloud of fresh smoke. Then he stood up.

"I think I get the story now," he said. "The missing pieces I can fill in later. You want me to take charge of the Terralune mines here on the Moon and try to get rid of this jinx, whatever it is. Well, maybe I can do it. The only question is, what do I get out of it?"

Ellen Bishop looked startled. "Get out of it? What do you mean?" she demanded. Then a scornful look came into her ice-blue eyes. "Oh, I see," she said. "Naturally, you feel that you've got us at your mercy. Well—"

Templin interrupted her. "I asked you a question," he reminded. "What do I get out of it?"

She smouldered. "Name your price," she said bitterly.

"Uh-uh." Templin shook his head. "I don't want money; I want something else."

"Something else?" she repeated in puzzlement. "What?"

Templin leaned across the desk. "I want to go back," he said. "I want a whole fleet of rocket ships to go back to Venus with me . . . lots of them, enough to start a colony. There's uranium on the Moon, and there are precious metals on Mercury . . . but on Venus there's something that's more important. There's a raw planet there, a whole world just like the Earth with trees, and jungles, and animals. And there isn't a human being on it. I want to colonize it—and I want Terralune Projects to pay the bill."

Ellen Bishop stared at him unbelievingly, and a slow smile crept into her lips. She said, "I beg your pardon . . . Temp. All right. It's a bargain." She grasped his hand impulsively. "If you can make the uranium mines pay out I'll see that you get your ships. And your colony. And I'll see that you can take anyone you like on the Terralune payroll along with you to get started."

"Sold," said Templin. He released her hand, wandered thoughtfully over to the huge picture window that formed one entire wall of the girl's room.

*   *   *

At a touch of his fingers the opaque covering on the window opened up like a huge iris shutter, and he was gazing out on the barren landscape of the Moon. The Dome was on the peak of Mt. Hadley, looking out on a desolate expanse of twisted, but comparatively flat, rock, bathed in a sultry dull red glow of reflected light from the Earth overhead. Beyond the plain was an awesome range of mountains, the needle sharp peaks of them picked out in brilliant sunlight as the Sun advanced slowly on them.

Culver said from behind him, "That's what they call the Sea of Serenity."

Templin chuckled. *"Mare Serenitatis,"* he said. "I know. I've been here before—fourteen years ago, or so."

Ellen Bishop amplified. "Didn't you know, Culver? Temp was one of Dad's crew when the old *Astra* landed here in 1957. I don't remember the exact order any more—were you the third man to step on the surface of the Moon, or the fourth?"

Templin grinned. "Third. Your father was fourth. First he sent the tw   Jnited Nations delegates off to make it all nice ana ιegal; then, being skipper of the ship, he was getting set to touch ground himself. Well, it was his privilege. But he saw me banging around the air lock—I was a green kid then—and he laughed and said, 'Go ahead, Temp,' and I didn't stop to argue." Templin sobered, and glanced at Ellen Bishop. "I've had other jobs offered me," he said, "and some of them sounded pretty good, but I turned them down. Maybe it isn't smart to tell you this, but there's nothing in the world that could make me quit the company your father founded. Even though he's dead and a debutante is running it now."

He grinned again at her, and moved toward the door. "Coming, Culver?" he asked abruptly. The tall man nodded and followed him. "So long," said Templin at the door, and closed it behind him without waiting for an answer.

2

They put on their pressure suits and stepped out of the lock onto the hard rock outside. Culver gestured and led the way to a small crater-hopping rocket parked a few hundred yards from the Dome. It was still eight days till sunrise, and overhead hung the wide, solemn disk of the Earth, bright enough to read by, big as a huge, drifting balloon.

Mount Hadley is thrust into the dry Sea of Serenity like an arrowhead piercing a heart. Like all the Moon's surface it is bare rock, and the tumbled mountain ranges that lie behind it are like nothing on the face of the Earth. Templin stared around curiously, remembering how it had seemed when that first adventuring flight had landed there. Then he loped over the pitted rock after Culver's swollen pressure suit.

Culver touched a key ring inset in the rocket's airlock, and the door swung open. They scrambled aboard, closed the outer door, and Culver touched a valve that flooded the lock with air. Then they opened the inner door and took off their pressure suits.

Culver said, "The Terralune mine is up at Hyginus

77

Cleft, about four hundred miles south of here. We'll
make it in twenty minutes or so.''

Templin sat down in one of the bucket seats before
the dual controls. Culver followed more slowly,
strapping himself in before he reached for the jet control levers. His ship was a little two-ton affair, especially
designed for use on the surface of the Moon; powered
with chemical fuel, instead of the giant atomics on
larger ships, it could carry two persons and a few hundred pounds of cargo—and that was all.

He fed fuel to the tiny jets, paused to give the
evaporators a chance to warm up, then tripped the
spark contact. There was a brief sputter and a roar. As
he advanced the jet lever a muffled grating sound came
from underneath, and there was a peculiar jolting,
swaying sensation as the rocket danced around on its
tail jets for a moment before taking off.

And then they were jet-borne.

Culver swept up to a thousand feet and leveled off,
heading toward a huge crater on the horizon. "My first
landmark," he explained to Templin.

Templin nodded silently, staring out at the horizon.
Although the sun itself was not yet visible, from their
elevation it was just below the horizon curve. As they
swept over a depression in the Moon's wrinkled surface
Templin caught a glimpse of unendurable brightness
where the sun was; a long, creeping tongue of flame that
writhed in a slow snake curl. It was the sun's corona—a
rare sight on the Earth, but always visible on the Moon,
where there was no atmosphere to play tricks and blot it
out.

Culver said curiously, "I didn't know you were one
of the early Moon explorers. How come you aren't a
millionaire, like the rest of them?"

Templin shrugged. "I keep on the move," he said
ambiguously. "Yes, there were plenty of deals. I could
have claimed mining rights, or signed up for lecture
tours, or let some rocket-transport company pay me a
fat salary for the privilege of putting my name on their
board of directors. But I didn't want it. This way,

Terralune pays me pretty well for scouting around the Inner Planets for them. I just put the checks in the bank, anyhow—where I spend my time, you can't spend your money. Money doesn't mean anything on Venus.''

Culver nodded. His fingers danced skillfully over the jet keys as the nose of the rocket wavered a hair-breadth off course. Under control, the ship came around a couple of degrees until it was again arrowing straight for its target on the horizon, hurtling over the ancient, jagged face of the Moon.

Culver said casually, "I sort of envy you, Temp. It must be a terrific feeling to see things that no man has ever seen before. I guess that's why I came to the Moon, looking for things like that. But heaven knows, it's getting more like Earth—and the slums of the Earth, at that—every day. Ever since they put that Dome on Mount Hadley the place has been crummy with billionaire tourists.''

Templin nodded absently. His attention was fixed on the rear-view periscope. He frowned. "Culver," he said. "What's that coming up behind us?"

Culver glanced at the scope. "Oh, that. Pleasure rocket. Looks like Joe Olcott's ship—he's got about the biggest space-yacht around. Only his isn't really a pleasure ship, because he pulled some political strings and got himself a vice commander's commission in the Security Patrol, which means that his yacht rates as an auxiliary. No guns on it, of course; but the Patrol pays his fuel bills.''

"A sweet racket," said Templin. "But what the devil is he so close for? If he doesn't watch out he's going to get his nose blistered. Way he's going now he'll be blasting right into our rocket exhaust.''

Culver stared worriedly at the periscope. The fat bullet-shaped rocket yacht behind them was getting bigger in the scope, little more than a mile behind them. Then he exhaled. "There he goes," said Culver. The other ship swung its nose a few degrees off to the west. It was a big fast job, burning twice as much fuel as their light crater-jumper, and it slid past them not more than a quarter of a mile away, going in the same direction.

"Joe Olcott," said Templin. "I begin to think that I'm not going to like Mr. Olcott. And I'm pretty sure he doesn't like me; his jaw will be sore for a day or two to help him remember."

Culver grinned and fumbled in his pockets for a cigarette. "He's one of the billionaire tourists I was telling you about, Temp," he said. He sucked on the cigarette, puffed out blue smoke which the air purifiers drew in. "Olcott's about the worst of the bunch, I guess. Not only is he a rich man, but he's mixed up in—Hey! What're you doing?"

Culver squawked in surprise as Templin, swearing incandescently, dove past him to get at the jet controls. Then Culver's eyes caught what Templin had seen a fraction of a second earlier. The big, bullet-shaped rocket had passed them, then come around in a wide arc, plunging head-on at their little ship at a good fifty-mile-a-minute clip.

Templin, sputtering oaths, was clawing at the controls. Under his frantic fingers their ship came slowly over . . . too slowly. The bullet-shaped ship, carrying twice their jets, came at them until it was a scant hundreds of yards away. Then it switched ends in a tight 10-gravity power turn. When the steering jets had brought it around the space-yacht's pilot fed full power to his main-drive jets.

And deadly, white-hot gases from the rocket exhausts came flaring at Templin and Culver.

The little ship quivered in a death-agony. Templin, white-lipped and soundless now, did the only thing left to him. He cut every jet; the crater-jumper was tossed about in the torrent of flaming gasses from the other ship and hurled aside. The Moon's gravity drew it down and out of danger. Then Templin thrust over the main-drive jets again, checking their fall in a fierce deceleration maneuver. The impact almost blanked Culver out; for a moment dark red specks floated before his eyes.

When his vision cleared, he found them settling on their jets in the middle of a five-acre rock plain that formed the center of a small crater.

Templin fought the controls until the landing-struts touched rock. Then he cut jets; the swaying, unstable motion ceased and they were grounded.

Culver shook his head dazedly. "What the devil happened?" he gasped.

"Wait!" Templin's voice was urgent. Culver looked at him in astonishment, but held his tongue. Templin sat stock-still for a second, his bearing one of extreme concentration. Then he relaxed. "Don't hear any escaping air," he reported; "I guess the hull's still in one piece." He peered through the vision port at the black star-filled sky overhead. The long trail of rocket flame from the other ship came around in a sweeping curve that circled over them twice. Then, apparently satisfied, the other pilot straightened out. The flame trail pointed straight back the way they had come as the space-yacht picked up speed. In a moment it was out of sight.

Templin smiled a chill smile. "He thinks he got us," he said. "Let him go on thinking so—for now."

"Tell me what that was all about," Culver demanded. "Two years I've been on the Moon, and nothing like this has ever happened to me before. What in heaven's name was he trying to do?"

Templin looked at him mildly. "Kill us, I should think," he said. "He came close enough to it, too."

"But why?"

Templin shrugged. "That's what I mean to find out. It might be because he's the man I slugged back in the Dome—but I doubt it. Or it might be because he thinks I can put Terralune's mine back on its feet. Wish I shared his confidence."

He unbuckled his safety straps and stood up. "This tub got a radio?" he demanded.

Culver, still pondering over what he had said, looked at him glassily a second. "Radio? Oh—no, of course not. Ship radios don't work on the Moon. You should know that."

Templin grinned. "When I was here there weren't any other ships to radio to. *Why* don't ship radios work?"

"Not enough power. It's not like the Earth, you know—any little one-watt affair can broadcast there, because the signals bounce off the Heaviside Layer. But you can't radio to anything on the Moon unless you can see it, because there isn't any Heaviside Layer to reflect radio waves, and so they only go in straight lines."

"How about the radio at the Dome?"

Culver shrugged. "That's a big one; that one bounces off the Earth's Heaviside Layer. What do you want a radio for, anyhow?"

"Wanted to save time," Templin said succinctly. "No matter. Come on, we've got a job of inspection to do. Put on your pressure suit."

Culver began complying automatically. "What are we going to do?"

"Make an external inspection. Way we were being kicked around up there, I want to make sure our outside hull is okay before I take this thing up again. Let's go look."

The two men slipped into air-tight pressure suits, sealed the helmets and stepped lightly out onto the lunar surface.

Templin skirted the base of the rocket, carefully examining every visible line and marking on the metal skin with the help of a hand-light. Then he said into his helmet radio, "Looks all right, Culver. By the way, what's that thing over there?"

He pointed to something that gleamed, ruddily metallic, at the base of the crater wall. Culver followed the direction of his arm.

"That's a rocket-launching site," he said. "Good place to stay away from. It's a hangover from the Three-Day War—you know, when the boys got the idea they could conquer Earth by blasting it with atom-rockets from the Moon."

Templin nodded. "I remember," he said grimly. "My home town was one of the first cities wiped out.

But why is it a good place to avoid?''

Culver scowled. "Wild radiations. They had a plutonium pile to generate power, and in the fighting the thing got out of control and blew its top. Scattered radioactive matter for half a mile around. Most of it's dead now, of course—these isotopes have pretty short half-lives. But the pile's still there.''

Templin said: "And there it can stay, for all of me. Well, let's get moving. The ship looks intact to me—if it isn't, we'll find out when we put the power on.''

Culver followed him into the ship's tiny pressure chamber. When they were able to take their helmets off he said curiously, "What's your next move, Temp? Going to get after Olcott?''

"That I don't know yet. One thing is for sure—that was no accident that just happened; he really wanted to blast us. And he had the stuff to do it with, too, with that baby battleship he was flying. It wasn't his fault that we ducked and only got a little dose of the tail end of his rocket blast. . . . Get in the driver's seat, Culver. The sooner we get to the mine, the sooner the next round starts!''

Three hours later, Templin was down in the mine galleries at Hyginus Cleft, staring disgruntedly at the wreck of a Mark VII digging machine. This was Gallery Eight richest vein of uranium ore they had found; just when the Mark VII had really begun to turn out sizeable amounts of metal there had been a shift in the rock underneath, crumbling the supports and bringing the shaft's ceiling down to pin the machine. Now the Mark VII, looking like a giant, steel-clad bug on its glittering caterpillar treads, was just half a million dollar's worth of junk.

Culver told him, "Tim Anson, here, was running the machine when the cave-in started; he can tell you all about it.''

Templin looked at the man Culver had indicated, a short space-suited figure whose face was hidden behind an opaque mask. The mines were worked in vacuum, of course; it would have been impossible to keep the shafts filled with air. And the dangerous radiations present in the uranium ore required a special helmet for all who stayed long within range of them—a plastic material that transmitted light and other harmless rays in only one direction; dangerous rays it did not transmit at all. Templin said, "What about it, Anson? What happened?"

The man's voice came into his helmet radio. "There's nothing much to tell, sir," it said. "We opened this shaft 'bout a week ago and got some very pretty samples out of it. So we put the Mark Seven in, and I was on it when all of a sudden it began to shake. I thought the machine had gone haywire somehow, so I shut it off. But the shaking kept up, so I hopped off and beat it toward the escape corridor. And then the roof came down. Good thing I was off it, too; smashed the driver's seat like a tin toy."

Templin scowled. "Don't you survey these galleries?" he demanded of Culver. "If there was a rock fault underneath, why didn't you find out about it before you brought the Mark Seven down?"

Culver spread his hands. "Believe it or not, Temp, we surveyed. There *wasn't* any fault."

Templin glared at him. Before he could speak, though, a new voice said tentatively, "Mr. Templin? Message from the radio room." It was another miner holding a sheet of thin paper in his gauntleted hand. Templin took the flimsy from him and held it up to his faceplate. In the light of the helmet lamp he read:

Pilot Rocket Silvanus registry Joseph Olcott reported accident as required by Regulations. Report stated your Rocket not seen until collision almost inevitable then evasive action taken but impossible to avoid rocket exhaust striking your ship. Pilot reprimanded and cautioned. Signed: Stephens, HQ Lunadmin Tycho Crater.

Templin grinned leanly and passed the radio from

Lunar Administration over to Jim Culver. "I squawked to Tycho about our little brush with Olcott," he explained.

Culver read it quickly and his face darkened with anger. Templin said over the inter-suit radio: "Don't get excited, Culver—I didn't expect anything better. After all, it stood to reason that Olcott would report it as an accident. He had to, in case we survived. At least, now we know where we stand." He glanced around the mine gallery, then frowned again. "I've seen enough," he said abruptly. "Let's go upstairs again."

Culver nodded and they walked back to the waiting monorail ore car. They stepped in, pressed the release button and the tiny wheels spun round. The car picked up speed rapidly; half a minute later it slowed and stopped at the entrance to the shaft. They crossed an open space, then walked into the air lock of the pressurized structure where Terralune's miners lived.

In the office Templin stripped off his pressure suit and immediately grabbed for one of his cigarettes. Culver more slowly followed his example, then sat down facing Templin. "You've seen the picture now, Temp," he said. "Do you have any ideas on what we can do?"

Templin grimaced. "In a negative sort of way."

"What do you mean?"

"Well, up to a little while ago I had a pretty definite idea that it was Joe Olcott who was causing all our trouble. That, I figured, I could handle—in fact, you might say I was sort of looking forward to it. But although Olcott is a rich and powerful man and all that, I don't see how he can cause earthquakes."

Culver nodded. "That's it," he said soberly. "That's not the first time it's happened, either. We've had other kinds of trouble—broken machinery, mistakes in judgement, that sort of thing. Like you, I thought Olcott might be behind it. But—well, good Lord, Temp. The Moon is an old, old planet. There isn't even any internal heat any more—it's all cooled off, and you'd think that its crust would have finally settled by this time. And yet . . . earthquakes keep on happening. Five of them so far.''

Templin grunted and chucked away his cigarette. ''Get the strawbosses in here,'' he said. ''Let's have ourselves a conference; maybe somebody will come up with an idea.''

Culver flicked on a communicator and spoke into it briefly. He made four or five calls to different stations on the intercom set, then turned it off. ''They'll all be here in about five minutes,'' he reported.

''Okay,'' said Templin. He pointed to a map on the wall behind Culver. ''What's that?'' he asked.

Culver turned. ''That's the mine and environs, Temp. Right here''—he placed his finger on the map—''is the living quarters and administration building, where we are. Here's the entrance to the shafts. Power plant —that's where the solar collectors are. You know we pick up sunlight on parabolic mirrors, focus it on a heat exchanger and use it to generate electricity. This over here is the oxygen plant.''

''You mean, we make our own oxygen?''

''Well, sort of. There's a lot of quartz on the Moon's surface, and that's silicon dioxide, as you ought to know. We electrolyze it and snatch out the oxygen.''

Templin nodded. ''What about this marking up on top of the map?''

Culver grinned. ''That's our pride and joy here, Temp. It's an old Loonie city. Heaven knows how old—it's all run down into the ground now. Must be a million years old, maybe, but nobody knows for sure. But the Lunarians, whoever they were, really built for keeps—some of the buildings are still standing. Want to go over and take a look at it later?''

Templin hesitated. ''No, not today,'' he said regretfully. ''That's pleasure, and pleasure comes later.''

There was a knock on the door. Culver yelled, ''Come in,'' and it opened. A middle-aged, worried-looking man came in.

Culver introduced. him. "Sam Bligh," he said; "Sam's our power engineer."

Templin shook hands with Bligh, then with half a dozen other men who followed him through the door. When all were gathered he stood up and spoke to them.

"My name's Templin," he said. "I'm going to be running this project for a while. I didn't ask for the job, and I don't want it, but I seem to be stuck with it. The sooner we begin producing, the sooner you'll get rid of me." He looked around. "Now, one at a time," he said. "I want to hear your troubles . . ."

The conference lasted about an hour. Then Templin said his piece. "There's going to be some ore brought out in the next twenty-four hours," he said. "I don't care what we have to do to do it, but we are going to ship at least one shipload of the stuff this week. And two shiploads next week, and three the week after, until we're up to quota. That clear?" He looked around the room. The men in it nodded. "Okay," he said. "Let's get going."

3

Twenty-four hours later, according to the big Terrestrial clock that hung in the ebony sky, Templin stood space-suited at the portal of the mine and watched the first monocar-load of uranium ore come out. On the ground at his feet was a flat black box, the size of an overnight bag. When the hoist crews had unloaded the glittering fragments of ore and stowed them in the hold of a freight rocket, Templin said over the radio: "Hold it up, Culver; don't send the monorail back down. I want to take another look at Gallery Eight."

Culver, supervising the unloading, said, "Sure, Temp; I'll tag along with you." He sprang lightly into the monorail. Templin, picking up the black box, followed and they braced themselves for the acceleration.

As the car picked up speed, they hurtled down the winding mine tunnels, lighted only by the headlights of the car itself. Though there was no air to carry sound, they could feel the vibration of the giant wheels on the single metal track as a deep, shuddering roar. Then the roar changed pitch as the car's brakes were set by the braking switch at the end of the line. The car slowed and stopped.

They got off and stepped down the rough-hewn gallery to where eight workmen were half-heartedly trying to clear the rock from the pinned Mark VII digging machine.

They stopped work to look at Templin. Templin said, "Go ahead, boys; we're just looking around." He moved toward the Mark VII, Culver following, studying the cave-in. Gallery Eight was seven hundred feet below the surface of the Moon, which meant that, even under the light gravity conditions prevailing on the satellite, there were many millions of tons of rock over their heads.

Frowning, Templin saw that there were strain-cracks on the tunnel walls—deep, long cracks that ran from floor to ceiling. They seemed to radiate from the point where the digging machine had been pinned down.

One of the workmen drifted over, watching Templin curiously. Templin glanced at the man, then turned to Culver. "Take a look at this," he ordered.

Culver looked indifferently. "Yeah. That's where the rock cracked and pinned down the machine."

"Uh-uh." Templin shook his head. "You've got the cart before the horse. Those cracks *start* at the mining machine. First the machine broke through, *then* the walls cracked."

Culver gaped at him through the transparent dome of his pressure suit. "So what?"

Templin grinned. "I don't know yet," he confessed; "but I aim to find out."

He picked up the case he had been carrying, opened it. Inside was a conglomeration of instruments—dials, meters, what looked like an old-fashioned portable radio, complete with earphones. These Templin disconnected, plugging the earphone lead into a socket on his collar-plate that led to his suit radio.

Culver's eyes narrowed curiously, then his expression cleared. "Oh, I get it," he said. "That's a sound-ranging gadget. You think—"

"I think maybe there's something wrong below," Templin cut in. "As I said yesterday, it looks to me as though there's a rock fault underneath here. That machine broke through the floor of the tunnel. When you consider how light it is, here on the Moon, that means that there was one damn thin shell of rock underneath it. Or else—well, I don't know what else it could be."

Culver laughed. "You'd better start thinking of something, Temp. That floor was solid; I know, because I handled the drilling on this gallery, and I was pretty careful not to let the Mark Seven come in until I'd sound-ranged the rock myself. Look—I've got the graphs back in the office. Come back and I'll show them to you."

Templin hesitated, then shook his head. "You might have made a mistake, Culver. I—I might as well tell you, I checked up on you. I looked over the sound-ranging reports last night. According to them, it's solid rock, all right—but still and all, the Mark Seven crashed through." He bent down, flipped the starting switch on his detection device. "Anyway, this will settle the question once and for all."

Inside the satchel-like instrument, an electronic oscillator began sending out a steady beat, which was picked up by a sound-reflector and beamed out in a straight line. An electric "ear" in the machine listened for echoes, timed them against the sending impulse and in that way was able to locate very accurately the distance and direction of any flaw in the rock surrounding them.

The machine was sensitive enough to tell the difference between dry and oil-bearing strata of sand—it had been used for that work on Earth. And for it to recognize a cave in the solid rock of the Moon was child's play. So simple, and so hard to mistake, that Templin avoided the question of how the first reports, based on Culver's tests, could have been wrong. The machine could not be mistaken, Templin knew. Could the men who operated it have been treacherous?

Templin pointed the reflector of the instrument at the rock under the trapped Mark VII and reached for the control that would permit him to listen in on the tell-tale echoes from below.

Culver, watching Templin idly, saw the abrupt beginnings of a commotion behind him. The eight workmen who were clustered around the Mark VII suddenly dropped their tools and began to stampede toward them, puffy arms waving wildly and soundlessly.

"What the devil!" ejaculated Culver. Templin glanced up.

Then they felt it, too. Through the soles of their metal-shod feet they felt a growing vibration in the rock. Something was happening—something bad. They paused a second, then the workmen in their panicky flight came within range of their suit radios and they heard the words, *"Cave-in!"*

Templin straightened up. Ominously, the cracks in the wall were widening; there was a shuddering uneasiness in the feel of the rock floor beneath them that could mean only one thing. Somehow, the rockslide that had wrecked the Mark VII earlier was being repeated. Somewhere beneath their feet a hole in the rock was being filled—and it might well be their bodies that would fill it.

Cursing, Templin jumped aside to let the panic-stricken workmen dash by. Then, half-dragging the paralyzed Culver, he leaped for the monorail car to the surface. They were the last ones on, and they were just barely in time. The stampeding miners had touched the starting lever, and the monorail began to pick up speed under them as they scrambled aboard.

Looking dazedly behind as the monorail sped upward, Templin saw the roof of the tunnel shiver crazily, then drop down, obliterating the wrecked Mark VII from sight. Luckily, the cave-in spread no farther, but it was a frightful spectacle, that soundless, gigantic fall of rock.

And all the more so because, just as the roof came

down on the digging machine, Templin saw a figure in
pressure suit and opaque miner's helmet dash from the
back of the machine to a sheltering cranny in the gallery
wall. The man was trapped; even if there had been a way
to stop the monorail and go back for a rescue try, there
was no way of getting to him, through the thousands of
cubic yards of rock that fell between, in time to save a
life . . .

Up in the office, Templin was a caged tiger, raging as
he paced back and forth. His stride was a ludicrous
slow-motion shamble in the light gravity, but there was
nothing ludicrous about his livid face.

He stopped and whirled on Culver. "Eight men down
in that pit—and only seven of them got out! One of our
men killed—half a million dollars worth of equipment
buried—and why? Because some fool okayed the
digging of a shaft directly over an underground cave!"

Culver shifted uncomfortably. "Wait a second,
Temp," he begged. "I swear to you, there wasn't any
cave there! Take a look at the sound-ranger graphs
yourself."

Templin dragged in viciously on a cigarette. He
exhaled a sharply cut-off plume of smoke, and when he
answered his voice was under control again. "You're
right enough, Culver," he said, "I've looked at the
things. Only—there *was* a cave there, or else the miner
wouldn't have fallen through. And how do you explain
that?"

The door to the office opened and the personnel clerk
stuck a worried head in. "I checked the rosters, Mr.
Templin," he said.

Templin's jaw tensed in anticipation. "Who was
missing?" he asked.

"That's the trouble, sir; no one is missing!"

"What!" Templin stared. "Look, Henkins, don't
talk through your hat. There were eight miners down in
that pit. Only seven came out. I *saw* one of them left
behind, and there isn't a doubt in the world that he's
still there dead. Who is it?"

The clerk said defensively, "I'm sorry, Mr. Templin. There are four men in the powerplant, five guards patrolling the shaft and area and two men on liberty at Tycho City. Every one of them is checked and accounted for. Everybody else is right here in the building." He went on hastily, before Templin could explode: "But I took the liberty of talking to one of the miners who was down there with you, Mr. Templin. Like you, he said there were eight of them. But one man, he said, wasn't part of the regular crew. He didn't know who the odd man was. In fact"—Henkins hesitated—"he thought it was *you*!"

"Me? Oh, for the good Lord's sake!" Templin glared disgustedly. "Look, Henkins, I don't care what your friend says—that man was part of the regular crew. At least he was a miner from this project—he had an opaque miner's helmet on; I saw it myself. You find out who he was, and don't come back here until you know."

"Yes, Mr. Templin," said Henkins despairingly, and he closed the door gently behind him.

Templin threw away his cigarette. "I would give five years' pay," he said moodily, "to be back on Mercury now. There I didn't have any troubles. All I had to worry about was keeping from falling into lava pits, and staying within sight of the ship."

Culver leaned back against the steel wall of the office. "Sounds fun," he said.

A buzzer sounded. Wearily Templin spoke into the teletone on his desk. "Hello, hello," he growled.

The voice that came out was the worried voice of Sam Bligh. It said, "Trouble, Templin. Something's happened to our energy reserves. The power leads are short-circuited. Can't tell what caused it yet—but it looks like sabotage."

The giant parabolic mirrors were motionless as Culver and Templin approached them, pointed straight at the wide disk of the Earth hanging overhead. The two men glanced at them in passing, and hastened on to the low-roofed power building. Bligh was waiting for them inside. With a sweep of his arm he indicated the row of power meters that banked the wall.

"Look!" he said. "Every power pack we had in reserve—out. There isn't a watt of power in the project, except what's in the operating condensers." Templin followed the direction of his gesture, and saw that the needle on each meter rested against the "zero" pin.

"What happened?" Templin demanded.

Bligh shrugged helplessly. "See for yourself," he said. He pointed to a window looking down on the generating equipment buried beneath the power shack itself. "Those square contraptions on the right are the mercury-laminate power packs. The leads go from the generators to them; then we tap the packs for power as we need it. Somehow the leads were cut about five minutes ago. Right there."

Templin saw where the heavy insulated cables had been chopped off just at the mixing box that led to the packs. He looked at it for a long moment, eyes grim. "Sabotage. You're right, Bligh—that couldn't be an accident. Who was in here?"

Bligh shook his head. "No one—as far as I know. I saw no one. But there wasn't any special guard; there never is, here. Anyone in the project could have come in and done it."

Culver cut in, "How long will the power in the condensor last?"

"At our normal rate of use—half a day; if we conserve it—a week. By then the sun will be high enough so that the mirrors will be working again."

"Working again?" repeated Templin. "But the generators are working now, aren't they?"

Bligh hesitated. "Well—yes, but there isn't enough energy available to make much difference. The Moon takes twenty-eight days to revolve, you know—that means we have fourteen days of sunshine. That's when we get our power. At 'night'—when the sun's on the other side—we turn the mirrors on the Earth and pick up some reflected light, but it isn't enough to help very much.''

Templin's face was gaunt in concentration. He said, ''Order the project to cut down on power. Stretch out our reserves as much as you can, Bligh. Culver—get a crew ready on one of the freight rockets.''

Culver raised his brows. ''Where are we going, Temp?''

Templin said, ''We're going to get some more power!''

Culver said tightly over Templin's shoulder, ''You realize, of course, that this is going to get us in serious trouble with the Security Patrol if they find out about it.''

''We'll try to keep that from happening,'' said Templin. ''Now don't bother me for a minute.'' His hands raced over the controls of the lumbering freight rocket. Underneath them lay the five-acre crater where they had crash-landed the day before after Olcott's attack. Templin killed the forward motion of the rocket with the nose jet, brought the nose up and set the ship down gently on the thundering fire of its tail rockets.

''Secure,'' he reported. ''Are the crew in pressure suits? Good. Get them to work.''

Culver sighed despondently and hurried off, shouting orders to the crew. Templin eased himself into his own suit. A hundred yards away lay the abandoned rocket-launching sites that had devastated a score of cities in the Three-Day War. Templin stepped out of the airlock and hastened after the group of pressure-suited men who were already investigating the ruined installation.

Culver waved to him. His voice over the radio was still disgusted as he said, ''There's the pile, Temp; this is your last chance to back out of this crazy idea.''

''We can't back out,'' Templin told him; ''we need power. We can generate power with our own uranium, if we take this atomic pile back with us and start it up again. Maybe it's illegal, but it's the only way we can keep the mine going for the next week—and I'm taking the chance."

"Okay," said Culver. He gave orders to the men, who began to take the ten-year-old piece of equipment apart. In their ray-proof miners' suits, they were in no danger from the feeble radioactivity still left after the pile had exploded. But Templin was, and so was Culver; their suits were the lighter surface kind, and they had to keep their distance from the pile itself.

A nuclear-fission pile is an elaborate and clumsy piece of apparatus; it consists of many hundreds of cubes of graphite containing tiny pieces of uranium, stacked together, brick on brick, in the shape of a top. There are cadmium control-strips for checking the speed of the nuclear reaction, delicate instruments that keep tabs on what goes on inside the structure, heavy-metal neutron shields and gamma-ray barriers and enough other items to stock a warehouse.

Looking it over, Culver grumbled: "How the devil can we get that heap of junk into the rocket?"

"We'll get it in," promised Templin. He bent down clumsily to pick up a rock, crumbled it in his gauntleted fist. It was like chalk. "Soft," he said. "Burned up by atomic radiation."

Culver nodded inside his helmet. "Happened when the pile blew up, during the War."

"No. It's like this all over the Moon, as you ought to know by now." Templin tossed the powdered rock away and brushed it off his space-gauntlets. "There's something for you to figure out, Culver. I remember reading about it years ago, how the whole surface of the Moon shows that it must have been drenched with atomic rays a couple of thousand years ago. The shape of the craters—the fact that the surface air is all gone—the big cracks in the surface—it all adds up to show that there must have been a terrific atomic explosion here once."

He glanced again at where the miners were disassembling the pile. "I kind of think," he said slowly, "that

that accounts for a lot of things here on the Moon. For one thing, it might explain what became of the Loonies, after they built their cities—and disappeared.''

Culver said, "You mean that you think the Loonies had atomic power? And—and blew up the Moon with it?''

Templin shrugged, the gesture invisible inside the pressure suit. "Your guess,'' he said, "is as good as mine. Meanwhile . . . here comes the first load of graphite bricks. Let's give them a hand stowing it in the rocket.''

Once the job of setting up the stolen plutonium pile was complete, Templin began to feel as though he could see daylight ahead. There was a moment of hysterical tension when the pile first began to operate with uranium taken from the mine—a split-second of nervous fear as the cadmium safety rods were slowly withdrawn and the atomic fires within the pile began to kindle—but the safety controls still worked perfectly, and Templin drew a great breath of relief. An atomic explosion was bad enough anywhere . . . but here, in the works of a uranium mine where the ground was honeycombed with veins of raw atomic explosive, it was a thing to produce nightmares.

After two days of operation the power-packs were being charged again and the mine was back in full-scale operation. Culver, seated in the office and looking at the day's production report, gloated to Templin, "Looks like we're in the clear now, Temp. Two hundred and fifty kilos of uranium in twenty-four hours—if we can keep that up for a month, maybe Terralune will begin to make some money on this place.''

Templin blew smoke at the white metal ceiling. "Don't count your dividends before they're passed,'' he advised. "The Mark VII is still out of operation—we won't be able to start any new shafts until we get a replacement for it, so our production is limited to what we can get out of Gallery Eight. And besides—we took care of our power problem for the time being, all right, but what about taking care of the man who caused it?''

"Man who caused it?'' repeated Culver.

"Yeah. Remember what Bligh said—that was sabotage. The leads were short-circuited deliberately.''

"Oh,'' Culver's face fell. "We never found out who the missing miner was, either,'' he remembered. "Do you—''

The teletone buzzed, interrupting him. When Templin answered, the voice that came out of the box was crisply efficient. "This is Lieutenant Carmer,'' it said. "Stand by for security check.''

"Security check?'' said Templin. "What the devil is that?''

The voice laughed grimly. "Tell you in just a moment,'' it promised. "Stand by. I'm on my way up.''

The teletone clicked off. Templin faced Culver. "Well?'' he demanded. "What is this?''

Culver said placatingly, "It's just a formality, Temp—at least, it always has been. The Security Patrol sends an officer around every month or so to every outpost on the Moon. All they do is ask a few questions and look to see if you've got any war-rocket launching equipment set up. The idea is to make sure that nobody installs rocket projectors to shoot at Earth with, as they did in the Three-Day War.''

"Oh? And what about our plutonium pile?''

Culver said sorrowfully, "That bothers me, a little. But I don't think we need to worry, because we've got the thing in a cave and so far they've never looked in the caves.''

"Well,'' said Templin, "all right. There's nothing we can do about it now, anyhow.'' He sat down at his desk and awaited his callers.

It only took a minute for the lieutenant to reach the office. But when the door opened Templin sat bolt upright, hardly believing his eyes.

The first man in was a trim, military-looking youth with lieutenant's bars on his shoulders. And following him, wearing the twin jets of a Security Patrol vice-commander, was the dark, heavy-set man with whom Templin had tangled in Hadley Dome, and whose ship had attacked them on the flight to the mine. Joe Olcott!

4

The lieutenant closed the door behind his superior officer and marched up to Templin. He dropped an ethergram form on Templin's desk. "My inspection orders," he said crisply. "Better look them over and see they're all right. I take it that you're the new boss around here."

Templin took his eyes off Olcott with difficulty. To the lieutenant he said noncommittally, "I run the mine, yes. Name's Templin. This is Jim Culver, works superintendent."

The lieutenant relaxed a shade. "We've met," he acknowledged, nodding to Culver. "I'm Lieutenant Garmer, and this is Commander Olcott."

Templin said drily, "I've met Mr. Olcott. Twice—although somewhat informally."

Olcott growled, "Never mind that; we're here on business."

"What sort of business?"

The lieutenant said hesitantly, "There has been a complaint made against you, Mr. Templin—a report of a violation of security regulations."

"Violation? What violation?" Templin reached casually for another cigarette as he spoke, but his senses were alert. This was the man with whom he had had trouble twice before; it looked like a third dose was in the offing.

Cramer looked at Joe Olcott before he spoke. "Plutonium, Mr. Templin," he said.

Culver coughed spasmodically. Templin said, "I see. Well, of course you can't take any chances, Lieutenant. Absurd as it is, you'd better investigate the report." To Culver he said: "Go up to the quarters and pick out two guides for them, Culver. They'll want to see our whole layout here; maybe you'd better go along too."

Culver nodded, his face full of trouble. "Okay, Temp," he said dismally, and went out.

Templin picked up the ethergrammed orders and read them carefully, stalling for time. They said nothing but what he already knew; they were typical military orders authorizing a party of two officers to inspect the Terralune Projects mine at Hyginus Cleft. He put it down carefully.

He got up. "Excuse me for a while," he said. "Culver will take care of you, and I've got a load of ore coming out to check. If you have any questions, I'll see you before you leave."

Olcott guffawed abruptly. "You bet you will," he sniggered, but he caught Templin's mild eyes and the laughter went out of him. "Go ahead," he said. "We'll see you, all right."

Templin took his time about leaving. At the door he said, "There are cigarettes on the desk; help yourselves." Then he closed the door gently behind him . . . and at once was galvanized into action. He raced to the metal climbing pole to the quarters on the upper level, swarmed up it at top speed and bounded down the galleyway, looking for Culver. He found Culver and two miners coming out of one of the rooms; he stopped them, took Culver aside.

"I need half an hour," he said. "Can you keep them away from the pile that long? After that—I'll be ready."

Culver said hesitantly, "I guess so. But what's the deal, Temp?"

"You'll find out," Templin promised. "Get going!"

Templin took three men and got them into pressure suits in a hurry. They didn't even take time to pump air out of the pressure chamber; as soon as the inner door was sealed, Templin slammed down the emergency release and the outer door popped open. The four of them were almost blasted out of the lock by the sudden rush of air under normal pressure expanding into the vacuum outside. It was a waste of precious oxygen—but Templin was in a hurry.

The stars outside were incandescent pin-points in the ebony sky. Off to the west the tops of the mountains were blinding bright in the sun, but it was still night at the mine and the huge Earth hung in the sky overhead.

They leaped across the jagged rock, heading toward the abandoned shaft in which lay the plutonium pile Templin had stolen. As they passed the gleaming mirrors of the solar-energy collectors Templin glanced at them and swore to himself. Without the pile's power to recharge their power-packs they were dependent on the feeble trickle of Earthshine for all their power—far less than the elaborate power-thirsty equipment of the mine needed. But there was no help for it. Perhaps, when Olcott and the security lieutenant had gone, they could revive the pile again and resume mining operations; until then, there would be no power, and mining operations would stop.

Hastily he set two of the men to digging up and rechanneling the leads to the power dome. Templin and the other man scuttled down into the yawning black shaft.

In the darting light of his helmet lamp he stared around, calculating the risks for the job in hand. The pile had to be concealed; the only way to conceal it was to blast the mouth of the tunnel shut. The pile itself was made of sturdy stuff, of course, with its ray-proof shielding and solid construction. But certainly operation of the pile would have to stop while Olcott and the lieutenant were in the vicinity, for the tiny portable Geiger counters they carried would surely detect the presence of a working atomic pile, no matter how thick and thorough the shielding.

And once a plutonium pile was stopped, it took hours to coax the nuclear reaction back to life. Any attempt to do it in a hurry would mean—atomic explosion.

Templin signaled to the workman, not daring to use his radio, and the two of them tackled the cadmium-metal dampers that protruded from the squat bulk of the pile. Thrust in as far as they would go, they soaked up the flow of neutrons; slowing down the atomic re-action until, like a forest fire cooled by cascading rain, the raging atomic fires flickered and went out. The reaction was stopped. The spinning gas-turbines of the heat-exchanger slowed and halted; the current generator stopped revolving. The atomic pile was dead.

On the surface, Templin knew, the current supply for the whole mining area was being shifted to the solar-energy reserves. The lights would flicker a little; then, as the automatic selector switches tapped the power packs, they would go back on—a little dimmer, no doubt.

Templin groaned regretfully and gestured to the other miner, who was throwing a heavy sheet-metal hook over the exposed moving parts of the generator. They hurried up and out to the surface.

Templin pulled a detonation-bomb from the cluster he had hung at his waist and, carefully gauging the distance, tossed it down the shaft. It struck a wall, rolled a dozen yards.

Then Templin flung himself away from the mouth of the shaft, dragging the other man with him. The bomb went off.

There was a flare of light and through the soles of their spacemen's boots they felt the vibration, but there was no sound. Templin saw a flat area of rock bulge noiselessly upward, then collapse. The entrance was sealed.

Grim-faced, Templin turned to await the coming of the inspection party. He had done all that could be done.

A miner, apparently one of the two who had been relocating the power leads, was standing nearby. Templin said curtly into the radio, "If you're finished, get back to the quarters." The man hesitated, then waved and moved slowly off.

Looking at the lights of the mine buildings, Templin could see that they were less bright now than before. Around the buildings small clusters of tinier lights were moving—the helmet lamps of pressure-suited men.

Looking close, Templin saw that three of the smaller lights were coming toward him—Culver, Olcott and the security lieutenant, he was sure. He gestured to his helper to keep out of sight and, in great swooping strides, he bounded toward the three lights.

As he got closer he could see them fairly clearly in the reddish light reflected from Earth overhead. They were the three he had expected, sure enough; they wore the clear, transparent helmets of surface Moon-dwellers, not the cloudy ray-opaque shields of the miners. He greeted them through his radio as casually as he could. "Find any plutonium?" he inquired amiably.

Even in the dim light he could see Olcott's face contort in a snarl.

"You know damn well we didn't," said Olcott. "But I know it's here; if I didn't have to be in Hadley Dome in two hours I'd stay right here until I found it!"

Templin spread his hands. "Next time, bring your lunch," he said.

The lieutenant spoke up. "We felt blasting going on, Templin," he said. "What was it?"

"Opening a shaft," Templin explained carefully; "we're in the mining business here, you know."

Olcott said, "Never mind that. Where are you getting your power?"

Templin looked at him curiously. "Solar radiation," he said. "Where else?"

"Liar!" spat Olcott. "You know that your sun-generators broke down! You don't have enough reserves to carry you through the night—" He broke off as he caught Templin's eye.

"Yes," said Templin softly, "I know we don't have enough reserves. But tell me, how did *you* know it?"

Olcott hesitated. Then, aggressively, "We—the Security Patrol has its way of finding things out," he said. "Anyway, that doesn't matter. I've been tracing your power lines out from the mine; if they end in solar generators, I'll admit we were wrong. I'm betting they end in a plutonium pile."

Templin nodded. "Fair enough," he said. "Let's follow the lines."

Olcott's rage when they came to the banks of light-gathering mirrors and photocells knew no bounds. "What the devil, Templin," he raged. "What are you trying to put over on us? Look at your power gauges—you haven't enough juice left there to electrocute a fly! Your reserves are way down—the only intake is a couple of hundred amps from the reflected Earthshine—and you're trying to make us think you run the whole mine on it!"

Templin shrugged. "We're very economical of power," he said. "Go around turning lights out after us, and that sort of thing."

The lieutenant had the misfortune to chuckle. Olcott turned on him, anger shining on his face. Templin stood back to watch the fireworks. Then . . . Olcott seemed, all of a sudden, to calm down.

He glanced at one of the miners, who had come up to join them, then at Templin. He pointed to the spot where Templin had just touched off the blast concealing the pile.

"What's over there?" he demanded triumphantly.

Templin froze. "Over where?" he stalled; but he knew it was a waste of time.

"Under that blasted rock," crowed Olcott. "You know what I'm talking about! Where you just blasted in the tunnel over your contraband plute pile!"

Templin, dazed and incredulous, stumbled back a step. How had Olcott stumbled on the secret? Templin could have sworn that a moment ago Olcott was completely in the dark—and yet—

Olcott snarled to the lieutenant, "Arrest that man! He's got a plutonium pile going in violation of security regulations!"

Hesitantly the lieutenant looked at his superior officer, then at Templin. He stepped tentatively toward Templin, arm outstretched to grab him . . .

Templin took a lightning-swift split-second to make up his mind, then he acted. He was between the other three men and the mine buildings. Beyond them was the Moon, millions of square miles of desolation. It was his only chance.

Templin plunged through the group, catching them by surprise and scattering them like giant slow-motion ninepins. Leaning far forward to get the maximum thrust and speed from his feet, he raced ahead, spanning twenty-foot pits and crevasses, heading for a crater edge where the rocks were particularly jagged and contorted. He was a hundred yards away, and going fast, before the three men could recover from their astonishment.

Then the first explosion blossomed soundlessly on a jagged precipice to his right.

It was the lieutenant's rocket pistol, for Olcott had none of his own—but Templin knew that it was the fat man's hand that was firing at him. Templin zigzagged frantically. Soundless explosions burst around him, but Olcott's aim was poor, and he wasn't touched.

Then Templin was behind the crater wall. He crashed into a rock outcrop with a jolt that sent him reeling and made him fear, for a second, that he had punctured the air-tightness of his helmet. But he hurried on, ran lightly for a hundred yards parallel to the wall, found a jet-black shadow at the base of a monolith of rock and crouched there, waiting.

There was no hiss of escaping air; his suit was still intact. After a moment he saw the lights of two men crossing the crater wall. They bobbed around for long minutes, searching for Templin. But there was too much of the Moon, too many sheltering hollows and impenetrable darknesses. After a bit they turned and went back toward the mine.

Templin gave them an extra five minutes for good measure. Then he cautiously crawled out of his hiding place and peered over the ridge.

No one was in sight, all the way to the mine buildings. He watched the lights of the buildings for a while, his face drawn with worry. The events of the last few moments had happened too rapidly to give him a chance to realize how bad a spot he was in. Now it was all coming to him. He had made a desperate gamble when he took the plutonium pile—and lost.

He stood there for several minutes, thinking out his position and what he had to do.

Then he saw something that gave him an answer to one of his problems, at least.

There was a sudden swelling burst of ruddy light that bloomed beyond the mine buildings, in the flat place where rocket ships landed. It got brighter, became white, then rose and lengthened into a sharp-pointed plume that climbed toward the tiny, bright stars overhead. It was the drive-jet off a rocket, taking off. Templin watched the flame level off, hurtle along at top speed in the direction of Tycho Crater.

It was the jet that had brought Olcott and the lieutenant, Templin was sure. They were going—but they would be back.

He hadn't much time. And he had a lot to do.

Taking no chances, Templin kept in the cover of the jagged rocks as he approached the dome. A few hundred yards from it he saw a pressure-suited figure moving toward him. He stood motionless in indecision for a moment, until he saw that the helmet on the figure was milkily opaque. A miner's helmet.

Templin stood up and beckoned to the figure. When it was within a few yards he said, "Have the Security Patrol officers gone?"

The miner stopped. Templin was conscious of invisible eyes regarding him through the one-way vision of the helmet. Then he heard a voice say: "Oh, it's you, Templin. I was wondering where you were."

Templin thought that there was something curious about the voice—not an accent, but a definite peculiarity of speech that he couldn't recognize. Almost as though the man were speaking a foreign language—

Templin glanced toward the dome and dismissed the thought. Someone was coming toward them; he had to make sure of his ground. He asked, "That rocket I saw—was that the Security Patrol? Have they both gone?"

"Yes."

"Fine!" Templin exulted. "Where's Culver, then?"

The figure in the space-suit gestured. Templin, following the pointing arm, saw the man who was coming toward them. "Thanks," he said, and raced to meet Culver, who was quartering off toward the power plant. Templin intercepted him only a short distance from the main building.

"Culver," he said urgently, "come into the dome. I've not got much time, so I've got to move fast. When Olcott and—" He broke off, staring. Culver was looking at him, his expression visibly puzzled even in the twilight, his mouth moving but no sound coming over the radio.

"What's the matter?" Templin demanded. Culver just stared. "Ahh," growled Templin, "your radio is broken. Come on!" He half-dragged Culver the remaining short distance to the dome. They climbed into the airlock, Templin closed the outer pressure doors and touched the valve that flooded the chamber with air. Before they were out of the lock Templin had his helmet off, was motioning to Culver to do likewise.

"What the devil was the matter with your radio?" he demanded.

"Nothing," said Culver in surprise. "It's yours that doesn't work."

"Well—never mind. Anyway, what happened to Olcott?"

"Took off for Tycho. Gone for a posse to hunt for you, I guess."

"Why didn't they radio for help?"

Culver grinned a little self-consciously. "That was me," he explained. "I—I told them we didn't have enough juice to run the radio. They didn't like it, but there wasn't anything they could do. We don't have very much power, and that's a fact."

Templin laughed. "Good boy," he said. "All right. Here's what I want to do. Olcott said he was going to Hadley Dome. I want to be there when he gets there. I think it's time for a showdown."

Culver looked forlorn, but all he said was, "I'll get a rocket ready." He went to the teletone in the anteroom, gave orders to the ground crew of the rockets. To Templin he said, "Let's go outside."

Templin nodded and got ready to put his helmet back on. As he was lifting it over his head something caught his eye.

"What the devil!" he said. "Hey, Culver. Take a look."

Culver looked. At the base of the helmet was a metal lug to which was fastened one of the radio leads. But the lug was snapped off clean; bright metal showed where it had connected with the helmet itself. The radio was broken.

Culver said in self-satisfaction, "Told you so, Temp; it was broken before, when I tried to talk to you outside."

Templin said thoughtfully, "Maybe so. Might have broken when I ran into that rock out at the crater—no! It couldn't have been broken. I was talking to a miner over it just before I met you."

"What miner?"

Templin stared at him. "Why, the one who left the building just before you did."

Culver shook his head. "Look, Temp," he said. "I had all hands in here when Olcott and the lieutenant took off. And I was the first one out of the place afterwards. There wasn't any miner."

Templin stood rooted in astonishment for a moment. Then he blinked. "I talked to *somebody*," he growled. "Listen, I've got twenty minutes or so before I have to take off. Let's go out and take a look for this miner!"

Culver answered by reaching for a suit. Templin picked another helmet with radio tap intact and put it on; they trotted into the pressure lock and let themselves out the other side.

Templin waved. "That's where I saw him." But there was no sign of the "miner".

Templin led off toward where the pressure-suited figure had seemed to be heading, out toward the old Loonie city. They scoured the jagged Moonscape, separating to the limit of their radio-contact range, investigating every peak and crater.

Then Culver's voice crackled in Templin's ear. "Look out there!" it said. "At the base of that rock pyramid!"

Templin looked. His heart gave a bound. Something was moving, something that glinted metallically and jogged in erratic fashion across the rock, going away from them.

"That's it!" said Templin. "It's heading toward the Loonie city. Come on—maybe we can head him off!"

The thing went out of sight behind an outcropping of rock, and Templin and Culver raced toward it. It was a good quarter mile away, right at the fringe of the Loonie city itself. It took them precious minutes to get there, more minutes before they found what they sought.

Then Templin saw it, lying on the naked rock. "Culver!" he whooped. "Got it!"

They approached cautiously. The figure lay motionless, face down at the entrance to one of the deserted moon warrens.

Templin snarled angrily, "Okay, whoever you are! Get up and start answering questions!"

There was no movement from the figure. After a second Culver leaned over to inspect it, then glanced puzzledly at Templin. "Dead?" he ventured.

Templin scowled and thrust a foot under the spacesuit, heaved on it to roll it over.

To his surprise, the force of his thrust sent the thing flying into the air like a football at the kick. Its lightness was incredible. They stared at it open-mouthed as it floated in a high parabola. As it came down they raced to it, picked it up.

The helmet fell off as they were handling it. Culver gasped in wonder.

There was no one in the suit!

Templin said, "Good lord, Culver, he—he took the suit off! But there isn't any air. He would have died!"

Culver nodded soberly. "Temp," he said in an awed voice, "just *what* do you suppose was wearing that suit?"

5

Templin jockeyed the little jet-ship down to a stem landing at the entrance to Hadley Dome, so close to the Dome itself that the pressure-chamber attendant met him with a glare. But one look at Templin's steel-hard face toned down the glare, and all the man said, very mildly, was, "You were a little close to the Dome, sir. Might cause an accident."

Templin looked at him frigidly. "If anything happens to this rathole," he said, "it won't be an accident. Out of my way."

He mounted the wide basalt stair to Level Nine and pounded Ellen Bishop's door. A timid maid peeped out at Templin and said: "Miss Bishop is upstairs in the game room, sir. Shall I call her on the Dome phone and tell her you're here?"

"Tell her myself," said Templin. He spun around and climbed the remaining flight of stairs to the top of Hadley Dome.

He was in a marble-paved chamber where a gentle fountain danced a slow watery waltz. To his right was Hadley Dome's tiny observatory, where small telescopes watched the face of the Earth day and night. Direc.ly ahead lay the game room, chief attraction of Hadley Dome for its wealthy patrons and a source of large-scale revenue to the billionaire syndicate that owned the Dome.

For Earthly laws did not exist on Hadley Dome; the simple military code that governed the Moon enforced the common law, and certain security regulations . . . and nothing else. Crimes of violence came under the jurisdiction of the international Security Patrol, but there was no law regulating drugs, alcohol, morals—or gambling. And it was for gambling in particular that the Dome had become famous.

Templin hesitated at the threshhold of the game room and stared around for Ellen Bishop. Contemptuously, his eyes roved over the clustered knots of thrill-seekers. There were fewer than fifty persons in the room, yet he could see that gigantic sums of money were changing hands. At the roulette table nearest him a lean, tired-looking croupier was raking in glittering chips of synthetic diamond and ruby. Each chip was worth a hundred dollars or more . . . and there were scores of chips in the pile.

Templin took his eyes off the sight to peer around for Olcott. The man was not in the room, and Templin mentally thanked his gods.

But at the far end, standing with her back to the play and looking out a window on the blinding vista of sun-tortured rock that was the Sea of Serenity, was Ellen Bishop, all alone.

Templin walked up behind her, gently touched her on the shoulder. The girl started and spun round like a released torsion coil.

"Templin!" she gasped. "You startled me."

Templin chuckled comfortably. "Sorry," he said. "Have you seen Olcott?"

"Why, no. I don't think he's in the Dome. But, Temp—what is the trouble at Hyginus? Culver radioed that the Security Patrol was after you for something! What is it?"

"Plenty of trouble," Templin admitted soberly. "And I only know one way out of it. Look, Ellen —don't ask questions right now; there are too many people around here, with too many ears. And I want you to do something."

He glanced around the room, selected a dice table that had a good view of the door. "Let's risk a few dollars," he suggested. "I have a feeling that this is my lucky night!"

Templin played cautiously, for the stakes were too high for any man on a salary to afford. But by carefully betting against the dice and controlling the impulse to pyramid his winnings, he managed to stay a few chips ahead of the game.

Ellen, scorning to play, was fuming beside him. She said in a vicious whisper, "Temp, this is the most idiotic thing I ever heard of! Don't you know that the Patrol is after you? Olcott comes here every night; if he sees you—it's all up!"

Templin grinned. "Patience," he said. "I know what I'm doing. Give you six to five that the man doesn't make his eight."

Ellen tossed her head. "Too bad," said Templin. "I would have won." The dice passed to Templin; he made one point, picked up his winnings, threw another and sevened out. He sighed and waited expectantly for the man beside him to bet.

Then—he saw what he was waiting for.

Joe Olcott appeared briefly in the door of the gambling salon. Templin spotted him at once and carefully took the opportunity to light a cigarette, screening most of his down-turned face with his hand. But it was an unnecessary precaution; Olcott was looking for someone else, a chubby little servile-looking man, who trotted up to him as soon as the big man appeared in the door. There was a brief whispered conversation, then Olcott and the chubby one disappeared.

Templin waited thirty seconds after they left. "I knew

it,'' he exulted. "Olcott said he was coming back
here—and I know why! Come on, Ellen—I want to see
where he's going."

Ellen stuttered protest but Templin dragged her out.
They followed the other two into the hall and saw that
the elevator indicator showed that the cage was on its
way down. "They're on it," said Templin. "Come
on—stairs are faster." He led the complaining girl down
the long basalt stairways at a precipitous pace. She was
exhausted, and even Templin was breathing hard, when
they rounded the landing to come to the last flight of
stairs. He slowed down abruptly, and they carefully
peeked into the lobby of Hadley Dome before coming
into sight.

Olcott's chubby companion had parted from him,
was disappearing down a long corridor that led to the
Dome's radio room. Olcott himself was putting on a
pressure suit, preparatory to going outside.

Templin halted, concealed by the high balustrade of
the stair. He nodded sharply, to himself. "This is it
Ellen," he said to the girl. "Something has been going
on—something so fantastic that I hardly dare speak of
it, far beyond anything we've dreamed of. But I think I
know what it is . . . and the way Olcott is acting makes
me surer of it every minute."

"What are you talking about?" demanded the girl.

Templin laughed. "You'll see," he promised.
"Meanwhile, Olcott's on his way to a certain place that
I want very much to see. I'm going after him; you stay
here."

Ellen Bishop stamped a foot. "I'm going along!" she
said.

Templin shook his head. "Uh-uh. You're not—that's
final. When this is over I'll be working for you
again—but right now I'm the boss. And you're staying
here."

He left her fuming and went out through the pressure
chamber, hastily tugging on the suit he had reclaimed

from the attendant. Templin had barely sealed the
helmet when the outer door opened, and vacuum sucked
at him.

He blinked painfully, staggered by the shock, as he
stepped out into the blinding fierce sun. In the days that
had passed since last Templin was at Hadley Dome, the
Moon's slow circling of the Earth had brought the
Dome into direct sunlight, agonizingly bright—hot
enough to warm the icy rock far above the boiling point
of water overnight. The helmet of his suit, even stopped
down as far as the polarizing device would go, still could
not keep out enough of that raging radiation to make it
really comfortable. But after a few moments the worst
of it passed, and he could see again.

Templin stared around for Olcott, confident that he
wouldn't see him . . . and he did not. Olcott was not
among the ships parked outside the Dome. Olcott was
out of sight around the Dome's bulk; Templin followed
and stared out over the heat-sodden Sea of Serenity.

Olcott's figure, bloated and forbidding-looking in the
pressure suit, was bounding clumsily down the long
slope of Mount Hadley, going in the general direction of
a small crater, miles off across the tortured rocky Sea.
Templin stared at the crater thoughtfully for a second.
Then he remembered its name.

"Linne," he said underneath his breath. "Yes!"
With a sudden upsurge at the heart he recalled the story
of Linne Crater—site of one of the biggest and least-
dilapidated Lunarian cities—the so-called "Vanishing
Crater" of the Nineteenth Century.

Templin nodded soberly to himself, but wasted no
more time in contemplation. Already Olcott was almost
out of sight, his bloated figure visible only when he
leaped over a crevasse or surmounted a plateau. It
would be easy enough to lose him in this jagged, sun-
drenched waste, Templin knew . . . so he hurried after
the other man.

Templin remembered the story of Linne, always an
enigma to Moon-gazers. It was Linne that, little more
than a century before, had been reported by Earthly

astronomers as having disappeared . . . then, a few years later in 1870, it had been discovered again in the low-power telescopes of the period—but with important changes in its shape.

What—Templin wondered abstractly—did those changes in its shape mean?

Obviously, Linne was their goal. It lay directly ahead in the path Olcott had taken, a good thirty miles away—across the roughest, most impassable kind of terrain that existed anywhere in the universe men traversed. A good three-day hike on Earth, it was only about an hour's time away on foot, on the light-gravitied surface of the Moon. But it would be an hour of sustained, strenuous exertion, and Templin gave all his concentration to the task of getting there.

A mile farther on, Templin glanced up as he cleared a hundred-foot-deep crevasse. Olcott's figure was nowhere to be seen.

Templin halted, a frown on his lean face. The fat man couldn't have reached the shelter of Linne crater yet—or could he? Had Linne been a wrong guess, after all—was Olcott's destination some place between?

Templin shrugged. Certainly Olcott was out of sight; it behooved Templin to get moving, to try to catch up.

He put his full strength into a powerful leg-thrust that sent him hurtling across a ravine and down into a shallow depression on the other side of it. As he balanced himself for the next leap . . .

Disaster struck.

Out of the corner of his eye, Templin saw a flicker of motion. A sprawling, spread-eagled figure in a pressure suit was sailing down on him from the lee of a small crater nearby; and from one of the outstretched hands glittered a brilliant, diamond-like reflection of sunlight on steel.

It was a spaceman's knife . . . and the man who bore it, Templin knew, was Olcott.

Templin writhed aside and out of the way of the knife, but the flailing legs of Olcott caught him and

knocked him down. Templin rolled like a ball, landed
on his feet facing the other man. Olcott's face behind
the clouded semi-opacity of the helmet was contorted in
hatred, and the long knife in his hand was a murderous
instrument as he leaped toward Templin again.

Templin paused a moment, irresolute. Olcott didn't
have a gun with him, he saw; if Templin chose, he could
take to his heels and Olcott wouldn't have a chance in
the world of catching him. But something within
Templin would never let him run from a battle . . . with
scarcely a second's hesitation, he grabbed for the dirk at
his own belt and faced his antagonist. If it was fight that
Olcott was after, he would give it to the man.

The two closed warily, eyes alert for the slightest
weakness on the other's part. Strange, deadly battle,
these two humans on the scared face of the Moon! In an
age of fantastic technological advance, it was to the
knife, after all, that humanity had returned for killing.
For nothing could be more deadly than a single tiny rent
made by one of these razor-sharp space knives in the
puffed pressure suit of an enemy. At the tiniest slit the
air would flood out, quick as bomb-flash, and the body
of the man inside would burst in horrid soundless explosion as the pressures within it sought to expand into
the vacuum.

Olcott drove a wicked thrust at Templin's mid-
section, which the bigger man parried with his steel
space-gauntlet. He dodged and let the chunky killer jerk
free. Templin's mind was clear, not masked by blinding
rage: he would kill Olcott if he had to, yes—but, if
possible, Templin would somehow disarm the other and
keep him alive.

Olcott feinted to the left, side-stepped and came in
with a shoulder-high lunge. Templin shifted lightly
away, then seized his chance; he ducked, dived inside
Olcott's murderous thrust, drove against him with the
solid shoulder of his pressure suit. The heavy-set man
puffed soundlessly, the wind knocked out of him, as he
spun away from the blow. Templin followed up with a
sledgehammer blow to the forearm; the knife flew out

of Olcott's hand, and Templin pounced.

He bore the other man down by sheer weight and impact, knelt on his chest, knife pressed against the bulge of the pressure suit just where it joined the collar. With his free hand he flicked on his helmet radio and said, "Give up, Olcott. You're licked and you know it."

Olcott's face was strained and suddenly as pale as the disk of the Moon itself. He licked his lips. "All—all right," he croaked. "Take that knife away, for the love of heaven!"

Templin looked at him searchingly, then nodded and stood up.

"Get up," he ordered. Olcott sullenly pushed himself up on one arm. Then, abruptly, a flash of pain streaked across his face. "My leg!" he groaned. "Damn you, Templin, you've broken it!"

Templin frowned and moved toward him cautiously. He bent to look at the leg, but in the shrouding bulkiness of the air-filled pressure suit there was no way for him to tell if Olcott was lying. He said, "Try and get up."

Olcott winced and shook his head. "I can't," he said. "It's broken."

Templin bent closer, suspiciously. "Looks all right to me—" he started to say. Then he realized his mistake—but too late to do him any good.

Olcott's other leg came up with the swiftness of a striking snake, drew back and lashed out in a vicious kick that caught Templin full in the ribs, sent him hurtling helplessly a dozen yards back. He wind-milled his arms, trying to regain his balance . . . but he had no chance, for at once the ground slid away from under him as he reeled backward into the yawning 500-foot crevasse, and down!

Lithe as a cat, Templin twisted his body around in space to land on his feet. The fall was agonizingly slow, but he still possessed all the mass, if not the weight, of his two hundred pound body, and if he struck on his helmet it would mean death.

He landed feet-first. The impact was bone-shattering, but his space-trained leg muscles had time to flex and cushion the shock. As it was, he blacked out for a moment, and came to again to looking up into a blinding sun overhead that silhouetted the head and shoulders of Olcott, peering down at him.

They looked at each other for a long moment. Then Templin heard the crackle of Olcott's voice in his helmet, and realized with a start that his radio was still working. "A hero," jeered Olcott. "Following after me single-handed. Sorry I couldn't let you come along with me."

Templin was silent.

"I'd like to ask you questions," Olcott continued, "but right now I haven't got time; I've got some urgent affairs to take care of."

"In Linne," said Templin. "I know. Go ahead, Olcott. I'll see you there."

Olcott's figure was quite motionless for a second. Then, "No," he said, "I don't think you will." And his head disappeared over the lip of the crevasse.

Templin had just time enough to wonder what Olcott was up to . . . when he found out.

A giant, jagged boulder, came hurtling down in slow motion from the edge of the chasm.

Slowly as it fell, Templin had just time enough to get out of its way before it struck. It landed with a shattering vibration that he felt through the soles of his feet, sending up splinters of jagged rock that splattered off his helmet and pressure suit. And it was followed by another, and a third, coming down like a giant deadly hail in slow motion.

Then Olcott's head reappeared, to see what the results of his handiwork has been.

Templin, crouched against a boulder just like the ones that had rained down, had sense enough to play dead. He stared up at Olcott with murder in his heart, disciplining himself, forcing himself not to move. For a long moment Olcott looked down.

Then Templin saw an astonishing thing.

Against the far wall of the crevasse, just below Olcott's head, a flare of light burst out, and almost at once a second, a few yards away.

Templin could see Olcott leap in astonishment, jerk upright and stare in the direction of Hadley Dome.

Someone was shooting a rocket pistol at Olcott. But whom?

Whoever the person was, he was a friend in need to Steve Templin. Olcott scrambled erect and disappeared; Templin waited cautiously for a long moment, but he didn't come back. Templin's unknown friend had driven the other man off, forced him to flee in the direction of the Loonie city at Linne Crater.

Templin, hardly believing in his luck, stood up. For several seconds he stood staring at the lip of the cleft, waiting to see what would happen.

A moment later a new helmet poked over the side of the chasm nearest Hadley Dome. Templin peered up in astonishment. It looked like—

It was.

The voice in his helmet was entirely familiar. "Oh, Temp, you utter idiot," it said despairingly. "Are you all right?"

It was Ellen Bishop. "Bless your heart," said Templin feelingly. "Of course I'm all right. Stand by to give me a hand—I'm coming up!"

6

It wasn't easy, but Templin finally managed to scramble out of the crevasse—after loping nearly half a mile along the bottom of it, to where the sides were less precipitous. Ellen Bishop, following his progress from above, was there to meet him as he clambered over the edge.

Remembering the genuine anxiety in her voice as it had come over the radio, he peered curiously at her face; but behind the shading helmet it was hard to read expressions. He smiled.

"You win another Girl Scout merit badge," he observed. "Whatever made you show up in the nick of time like that?"

Ellen's face colored slightly. "I was watching you," she said defiantly. "There's a spotting telescope in the Observatory at Hadley Dome and—well, I was worried about you. I went up and watched. I saw Olcott stop and look around, and then hide . . . so I figured out that he'd seen you. It looked like an ambush. And of course, you were such a big fool that you didn't take a rocket gun along with you."

"Couldn't afford to," Templin apologized. "Olcott's still in the Security Patrol—I didn't want to be caught following him with a gun tucked in my belt. Besides, he didn't have one himself."

"He had something," Ellen said. "Or did you just go down in that crevasse to look for edelweiss?"

Templin coughed. "Well," he said ambiguously. "As long as you're here, you might as well come the rest of the way." He craned his neck in the direction of the Loonie city, mockingly near now. Olcott was not in sight.

"Come on," he ordered. "Keep out of trouble, though. Olcott went a little too far when he jumped me. He can't turn back any more . . . and that means he's desperate."

The girl nodded. Side by side they drove on toward the solitary crater of Linne, alone in the middle of the Mare Serenitatis. Once Templin thought he saw Olcott's figure on top of a peak, watching them. But it didn't reappear, and he decided he had been mistaken. . .

They loped into the ancient city of the long-dead lunar race, Templin in the lead but the girl only a hair's-breadth behind. In the shadow of a giant ruined tower Templin gestured, and they came to a stop.

He switched off the transmitter of his helmet radio, motioned to the girl to do the same. When, somewhat puzzled, she obeyed, he leaned close to her, touching helmets.

"Keep your radio off!" he yelled, and the vibration carried his voice from his helmet to hers. "This is where Olcott's outfit hides out, whoever they are. If they hear our radios it'll be trouble."

Ellen nodded, and the two of them advanced down the broad street of the ravished Lunarian metropolis. Glancing at the shattered buildings all about them, Templin found his mind dwelling on the peculiar tragedy of the Moon's former inhabitants, who had risen from the animal, developed a massive civilization . . . and seen it wiped out into nothingness.

Ellen shuddered and moved closer to Templin. He understood her feeling; even to him, the city seemed haunted. The light of the giant sun that hung overhead was blinding; yet he found himself becoming jittery, seeing strange imaginary shapes that twisted and contorted in the utterly black shadows cast by the ruined walls.

They circled a shattered Coliseum, looking warily into every crevice, when Templin felt Ellen's gauntleted hand on his shoulder. He looked at her and touched helmets. Her face was worried. "Someone's watching us, Temp," she said positively, her voice metallic as it was transmitted by the helmets. "I feel eyes."

"Where?"

"How do I know? In that big round building we just passed, I think. It feels exactly as if they keep going around and around the building at the same time we do, always staying on the far side from us."

Templin considered. "Let's look," he said. "You go one way, I'll go the other. We'll meet on the other side."

"Oh, Temp!"

"Don't be frightened, Ellen. You have your gun—and I can take care of myself with my space knife."

Her lip trembled. "All right," she said. Templin watched her start off. She had drawn the gun and was holding it ready as she walked.

Templin went clockwise around the building, moving slowly and carefully, his hand always poised near the dirk at his belt. Almost anything might be lurking in the cavernous hollows in these old buildings. Olcott, he felt quite sure, *was* lurking somewhere nearby—and so were his mysterious friends. Templin stepped over a fallen carven pillar—strange ornamentation of curious serpentine beasts and almost-human figures straining toward the sky was on it—and froze as he thought he saw a flicker of motion out of the corner of his eye. But it was not repeated, and after a moment he went on.

He was clear back to his starting point before he realized that Ellen had disappeared.

Templin swore in the silence. There was no doubt about it. He had traveled completely around the circular building, and Ellen was gone.

He hesitated a second, feeling the forces of mystery gathering about him as they had about Ellen, then grimly dismissed the fantasy from his mind. There had to be a way of finding Ellen again . . . and at once.

His mind coldly alert, he circled the ancient Lunarian structure once more. Ellen was not in sight.

Templin stood still, thinking it over. Cautiously he retraced his tracks, eyes fixed on the soft Lunarian rock beneath him.

Fifteen yards away, he saw the marks of a scuffle on the ray-charred rock. Heavy space boots had been dragged there, making deep, protesting scars. Ellen.

Templin swore soundlessly and loosened his space knife in its scabbard. He stared up at the ruined Loonie temple. A crumbled arch was before him; inside the structure it disappeared into ultimate blackness. There was a curving corridor, heading downward in a wide spiral. He could see a dozen yards into it . . . then darkness obliterated his vision.

Templin shrugged and grinned tightly to himself. It looked so very much like a giant rattrap. Foolish, to go into unknown danger on the chance that Ellen was there—but it was the foolish sort of risk he had always been willing to take.

He snapped on his helmet lamp and stepped boldly in.

Down he went, and down. The corridor was roughly circular in section, slightly flattened underfoot and ornamented with ancient carvings. Templin flashed his light on them curiously as he passed. They were a repetition of the weirdly yearning figures he had seen on the columns outside—lean, tenuous man-like things, arms stretched to the sky. Curious, how like they were to human beings, Templin thought. Except for the lean-

ness of them, and the outsize eyes on the pearshaped
head, they could almost have been men.

Templin grimaced at them and went on.

He had walked about a mile in the broad, downward
spiral when he saw lights ahead.

Instinctively he snapped off his helmet lamp, stood
motionless in the darkness, waiting to see if he had been
noticed. But the lights, whatever they were, did not
move; he waited for long minutes, and nothing came
toward him. Obviously he had not been seen.

Templin cautiously moved up toward them, watching
carefully. They were too bright for helmet lamps, he
thought; and too still. But what other lights could be
down here in this airless cavern under the Moon? He
crept up behind a rock overhang and peered out.

"Good Lord!" Stunned Templin spoke aloud, and
the words echoed inside his helmet. For now he could
see clearly—and what he saw was unbelievable.

There were figures moving before the lights. A stocky
figure of a man in a pressure suit that Templin knew to
be Olcott, and others. And the other figures were—not
human!

Templin stepped out in the open to see more clearly.
Abruptly some atavistic sense made the hair on his neck
prickle with sudden warning of danger—but it came too
late. Templin whirled around, suddenly conscious of his
peril. Figures were behind him, menacing figures that he
could not recognize in the darkness, closing in on him.
He grabbed instinctively for his space knife, but before
he had it clear of its scabbard they were on him, bowling
him over with the force and speed of their silent attack.
He fell heavily, with them on top of him.

He struggled, writhing frantically, but there were too
many of them. They held him down; he felt hands
running over him, plucking his space knife from its
scabbard. Then he felt himself being picked up by a
dozen hands and carried face down toward the lights.

Templin made his mind relax and consider, fighting
to overcome his rage at being taken so by surprise. He

thought desperately of ruses for escape. . .

Then anger was driven out of his mind. He heard a thin, shrill whistle of escaping air within his helmet. It meant only one thing . . . his suit had been pierced in the struggle, and his precious air was leaking into the void outside.

He made a supreme, convulsive effort and managed to free one arm, but it was recaptured immediately and he was helpless. Templin groaned internally. He was a dead man, he knew—dead as surely as though the heart had been cut from his body. For his suit was leaking air and there was no way to stop it, no nearby pressure-dome into which to flee, nothing to do but die.

Templin resigned himself for death; he relaxed, allowing his captors to carry him along at a swift, jogging trot. His mind was strangely calm, now that death was so near. For anxiety and fright come only from uncertainty . . . and there was no more uncertainty . . . in Templin's mind.

He felt his captors drop him ungently on a rock floor. They were close to the lights now, he realized . . .

The hiss of air in his ears was gone. And he was still alive. Templin dazedly comprehended a miracle, for the air in his helmet and suit had leaked out until, somehow, it had established a balance. And that meant—

"Air!" He said it aloud, and the word was a prayer of thanksgiving. It was no less than a miracle that there should be air here, under the surface of the Moon—a miracle for which Templin was deeply and personally grateful.

Someone laughed above him. He scrambled to his feet uncertainly, looking up. It was Olcott, pressure-suited but holding his helmet in his hand, laughing at him.

Olcott nodded in grim humor. "Yes," he said, his voice coming thinly to Templin through his own helmet, "it's air all right. But it won't matter to you, because you aren't going to live to enjoy it. My friends here will take care of that!"

Olcott jerked a thumb toward the lights. Templin
followed with his eyes.

The lights were crude, old-fashioned electrics,
grouped in front of a pit that descended into the floor of
the cavern. And beyond the lights, standing in a stoic,
silent group, were a dozen lean figures, big-eyed, big-
headed, wearing brief loin-cloths of some mineral
material that glistened in the illumination.

Templin stared. For they were not human, those
figures. They were—the lean, questing figures that were
carved in the ancient Lunarian stone.

Templin forced himself to turn to Olcott. He glanced
at those who had captured him, half-expecting that they
would be more of the ancient, supposedly extinct
Lunarians. But again he was surprised, for the half-
dozen men behind him were as human as himself,
though pale and curiously flabby-looking. They wore
shredded rags of cloth that seemed to Templin to be the
remnants of a military uniform that had disappeared
from the face of the Earth years before.

Groping for understanding, Templin turned back to
Olcott. Then his mind cleared. There was one question
to which he *had* to know the answer.

"Where's Ellen Bishop?" he demanded.

Olcott raised his heavy brows. "I was about to ask
you that," he said. "Don't try to deceive me, Templin.
Is she hiding?"

Templin shrugged without replying.

Olcott waved. "It doesn't matter. She can't get away.
My patrols will pick her up—the Loonies are very good
at that."

Templin looked at the dark man's eyes. It was impossible to read his expression, but Templin decided
that he was telling the truth. There was no reason, after
all, for him to lie.

Templin said shortly, "I don't know where she is."
He pointed to the silent, watching figures beyond the
lights. "What are they?"

Olcott chuckled richly. "They're the inhabitants,

Templin. The original Lunarians. There aren't very many of them left—a thousand or so—but they're all mine.''

Templin shook his head. Hard to believe, that the ancient race had survived for so long underground—yet he could not doubt it, when his eyes provided him with evidence. He said, "What do you mean, they're all yours?"

"They work for me," said Olcott easily. He gestured sharply, and the scarecrow-like figures bowed and began to descend into the pit, by a narrow spiral ramp around its sides. "They're rather useful, in fact. As you should know, considering how much they've helped me at Hyginus Cleft."

"Sabotage—you mean—these things were—"

Olcott nodded, almost purring in satisfaction. "Yes. The—accidents—to your equipment, the damage to your generators and a good many other things, were taken care of for me by the Loonies. For instance, it was one of them who located your plutonium pile for me."

Templin scowled. "Wearing one of my miners' pressure suits, wasn't he? I begin to see." He looked at the group of pallid humans who had captured him. "They Loonies too?" he demanded.

Olcott shook his head. "Only by adoption," he said. "You see, they had the misfortune to be on the wrong side in the Three-Day War. In fact, they were some of the men who were operating the rocket projectors that were so annoying to the United Nations. And when your—*our*—compatriots began atom-blasting the rocket-launching sites, a few of them found their way down here." Olcott gazed at them benevolently. "They are very useful to me, too. They control the Loonies, you see—I think they must have been rather cruel to the Loonies when they first came, because the Loonies are frightened to death of them now. And I control *them*."

Templin stiffened. "Rocket projectors," he repeated. "You mean these are the men who bombed Detroit?"

Olcott waved. "Perhaps," he said. "I don't know which targets they chose. This may have been the crew that blasted Paris—or Memphis—or Stalingrad."

Templin looked at them for a long moment. "I'll remember," he said softly. "My family—never mind. What are you going to do with me?"

"I am very likely to kill you, Templin. Unless I turn you over to the Loonies for sport."

Templin nodded. "I see," he said. "Well, I—thought as much."

Olcott looked at him curiously. Then he issued a quick order to the pale, silent men behind him. It was not in English.

To Templin he said, "You shouldn't have gotten in my way. I need the uranium that your company owns; I plan to get it."

"Why?"

Olcott pursed his lips. "I think," he said, "that we will start the rocket projectors again. Only this time, there will be no slipups. As a high-ranking officer in the Security Patrol, I will make sure that we are not interfered with."

The pale men gripped Templin, carried him to the edge of the pit into which the Loonies had disappeared. Olcott said. "Good-by, Templin. I'm turning you over to the Loonies. What they will do to you I don't know, but it will not be pleasant. They hate human beings." He smirked, and added, "With good reason."

He nodded to the men; they picked Templin up easily, dropped him into the pit.

It was not very deep. Templin dropped lightly perhaps twenty feet, landed easily and straightened to face whatever was coming.

He was surrounded by the tall, tenuous Lunarians, a dozen of them staring at him with their huge, cryptic eyes. Silently they gestured to him to move down a shaft in the rock. Templin shrugged and complied.

He was in a rabbit-warren of tunnels, branching and forking out every few yards. Inside of a handful of minutes Templin was thoroughly confused.

They came to a vaulted dome in the rock. Still silent, the Lunarians gestured to Templin to enter. He did.

Someone came running toward him, crying: "Temp! Thank Heaven you're safe!"

Pressure suit off, dark hair flying as she ran to him, was Ellen.

Templin held her to him tightly for a long moment. When finally she stepped back he saw that her eyes were damp. She said: "Oh, Temp, I thought you were gone this time for sure! The Loonies told me that Olcott had captured you—I was so worried!"

Templin stared. "*Told* you? You mean these things can talk?"

"Well, no, not exactly. But they told me, all the same. It's mental telepathy, I suppose, Temp, or something very much like it. Oh, they can't read minds —unless you try to convey a thought—but they can project their own thoughts to another person. It sounds just like someone talking . . . but you don't hear it with your ears."

Templin nodded. "I begin to understand things," he said. "That miner at Hyginus—I thought I talked to him, and yet my radio was broken, so I couldn't have. And then, he abandoned his suit. Can the Loonies get along on the surface without pressure suits?"

Ellen looked uncertain. "I—I don't know. But—I think perhaps they can. They said something about Olcott forcing them to do it. Olcott has them under control, Temp. He's using them to get the uranium mines away from us—and the Loonies think he wants the uranium to make bombs!"

"I have heard about that," Templin said. "From Olcott. Which reminds me—how did you get down here without his knowing about it?"

Ellen said, "I was outside that Coliseum-looking place, up on the surface, and suddenly somebody grabbed me from behind. I was frightened half to death; he carried me down and through a bunch of tunnels to here. And then—why, this voice began talking to me, and it was one of the Loonies. He said—he said he wanted me to help him get rid of Olcott!"

Templin asked, "Why can't they get rid of him themselves? There are a couple thousand Loonies—and Olcott can't have more than fifteen or twenty men down here."

Ellen sighed. "That's the horrible thing, Temp. You see, these men haven't a thing to lose. When they came down here, they brought part of the warhead of an atom-rocket along. And they've got it assembled in one of the caverns, not far from here—right in the middle of a terrific big lode of uranium ore! Can you imagine what would happen if it went off, Temp? All that uranium would explode—the whole Moon would become a bomb. And that's what they're threatening to do if the Loonies try to fight them."

Templin whistled. He looked around the room they were in reflectively. It was a high-ceilinged, circular affair, cut out of the mother-rock, sparsely furnished with pallets and benches. Loonie living quarters, he thought.

He looked back at the hovering Lunarians, staring blankly at them from the entrance to the chamber. "How do you work this telepathy affair?" he demanded.

"Walk up to them and start talking. The effort of phrasing words is enough to convey the thought to them—as nearly as I can figure it out."

Templin nodded, looked at them again and walked slowly over. The bulbous heads with the giant eyes confronted him blankly. He said uncertainly, "Hello?"

A sensation of mirth reached him, as though someone had laughed silently beside his ear. A voice spoke, and he recognized its kinship to that of the "miner" he had stopped at Hyginus. It had the same curious strangeness, the thing that was not an accent but something more basic. It said, "Hello, Steve Templin. We have spared your life. Now tell us what we are to do with you."

"Why, I thought—" Steve stumbled. "That is, you're having trouble with these Earthmen, aren't you?"

"For sixteen of your years." There was anger in the thought. "We have not come to like Earthmen, Templin."

Templin said uncomfortably, "These Earthmen I don't like myself. Shall we make an alliance, then?"

The thought was direct and sincere. "It was for that that we spared your lives."

Templin nodded. "Good." Abruptly his whole bearing changed. He snapped: "Then help us get out of here! Get us back to Hadley Dome or Hyginus. We'll get help—and come back here and wipe them out!"

Regretfully, the Lunarian's thought came, "That, Templin, is impossible. Our people can go out into the vacuum unprotected, for short periods, but you cannot. Have you forgotten that your suit will no longer hold air?"

Templin winced. But he said, "Ellen's will. Let her go for help."

Wearily the thought came, "Again, no. For if you brought men here to help you the Earthmen who enslave us could not be taken by surprise. And if only one of them should live for just a few moments after the first attack . . . it would be the death of us all. They have hollowed out a chamber in the midst of a deposit of the metal of fire. They have said that if we act against them they will set off a chain reaction—and, in this, I know that they do not lie."

The Lunarian hesitated. Almost apologetically he went on: "It was from the metal of fire that the greatness of our race was destroyed many thousands of years ago, Templin. Once we lived on the surface, and had atomic power; because we used it wrongly we ravished the surface of our planet and destroyed nearly all of our people. Now—there are so few of us left, Templin, and we must not see it happen again."

Templin spread his hands. "All right," he said shortly. "What you say is true. But what do you suggest we do?"

The thought was sympathetic. "There is only one chance," it said. "If someone could enter the chamber of the bomb—my own people cannot approach, for it is not allowed. But you are an Earthman; perhaps you could reach it. And if you could destroy the men who are in there—the others we can account for.''

Templin gave it only a second's thought. He nodded reflectively. "It's the only chance," he agreed. "Well—lead the way. I'll try it."

The Lunarian peeped out into a corridor, then turned back to Templin. He said in his soundless speech, "The entrance to the room of power is to your right. What you will find there I do not know, for none of us have ever been inside."

Templin shrugged. "All right," he said. And to Ellen Bishop, "This is it; if I shouldn't see you again—it's been worthwhile, Ellen."

The girl bit her lip. Impulsively she flung her arms around him, hugged him tight for a second. Then she stepped back and let him go.

Templin stepped out into the corridor. No one was in sight. He patted the bulge of Ellen's rocket pistol where it was concealed under his clothing—he had taken off his pressure suit, torn the stout fabric of his tunic to match the ragged uniforms he had seen on the pale men—and turned down the traveled path to his right.

Thirty yards along, he came to a metal door.

A man was standing there, looking dreamily at the rock wall of the corridor. He looked incuriously at Templin but made no move to stop him. As Templin passed, the man said something rapid and casual to him in the language of the nation that had waged the Three-Day War.

That was the first hurdle. It didn't sound like a challenge, Templin thought, wishing vainly that he had learned that language at some time in his life. Apparently the fugitives had not considered the possibility of an inimical human being penetrating to this place.

Templin replied with a noncommittal grunt and walked on. The skin between his shoulder-blades crawled, expecting the blast of a rocket-shell from the guard. But it did not come; the thing had worked.

Templin found that he was in a room where half a dozen men sat around, a couple of them playing cards with what looked like a homemade deck, others lying on pallets that had obviously been commandeered from the Loonies.

Along one wall was an involved mechanical affair—a metal tube with bulges along its fifteen-foot length, and a man standing by a push-button monitor control at one end of it. That was his target, Templin knew. Built like an atom-bomb, it would have tiny fragments of uranium-235 or plutonium in it, ready to be hurled together to form a giant, self-detonating mass of atomic explosive at the touch of that button. And once the pieces had come together, nothing under the sun could prevent the blast.

The men were looking up at him, Templin saw. It was time to make his play. The thing was too much like shooting sitting ducks, he thought distastefully—yet he dared not warn them, give them a chance to fight back. Too much was at stake.

He gazed stolidly at the men who were looking at him, and his hand crept to where Ellen's rocket pistol was concealed inside his tunic.

"Templin!"

The shout was like a pistol-crack in his ears. Templin spun round frantically. And in the door stood Olcott, surprise and rage stamped on his face.

Templin whirled into action. The men in the room, abruptly conscious that something was wrong, were reaching for weapons. Templin made his decision and passed them up for the first shot—blasted, instead, the man at the atomic warhead control, most deadly to his plans. He saw the man's body disappear in incandescent red mist as the rocket shell hit, then fired at a clump of three who had weapons drawn, fired again and again. Surprise was with him, and he got each of them with his

potent shells. Yet—the odds were too much against him.
As he downed the last pale-skinned underground man,
Olcott was on him!

Templin reeled with the fury of his attack, grunted as
Olcott landed vicious stabbing blows on his unprotected
body. He lost control of the rocket-pistol in his hand,
saw it spin away across the room as Olcott thudded
against him with his steel-gauntleted hand. Templin
dropped to the floor under the pressure-suited body,
rolled and brought his knees up in a savage kick. The
chunky man grunted but lashed out and a steel fist
caught Templin at the base of the jaw. For a second the
chamber reeled around him. Another like that, he knew,
and he was done.

Olcott came down on him like a metal and fabric
colossus. The gauntleted hands reached for Templin's
throat and found it, circled it and squeezed. Templin,
battered and gasping in the thin air, found even that cut
off under the remorseless pressure from the other's
hands. He struggled with every trick he knew to break
the man's grip . . .

Blindly his hands reached out, closed on something,
heaved back. There was a sudden yielding, and Templin
felt air reach his lungs once more. But it came too late.

Darkness overcame him . . .

Someone was bending over him. Templin surged upward as soon as he opened his eyes. The figure leaped
away and emitted a slight shriek. "Temp!" it said
reprovingly.

Templin's eyes swam into focus again; it was Ellen.

He was in bed, in a huge room with filtered sunlight
coming in through a giant window. He was on the surface—by the look of it, back at Hadley Dome.

His head throbbed. He touched it inquiringly, and his
finger encountered gauze bandage. He stared at the girl.

"We won," she said simply. "The Loonies and I
came in as soon as we could—soon as we heard the
shooting. You did a terrific job, Temp. The only live

ones in the room were you and Olcott. And, just as we came in—Olcott died.''

"Died? Died how?''

"You broke his neck, Temp. He was strangling you, and you were fighting back, and you caught him under the chin and pushed. The metal collar of his pressure suit snapped his spine. And then, since you had a skull that's broken in three places, the surgeon says, you went off to sleep yourself.''

Templin shook his head incredulously. "And the Loonies?''

"They're free. And very grateful to you, too. They—they masacred all the other Earthmen, down under there. They'd been waiting for the chance for years, you see. And—well, you've been unconscious for two days, and I've been busy. Things are under control now. The mine is back in operation—Culver's outside, waiting to see you—and you're free, too, Temp. You can go back to the Inner Planets whenever you like.''

Templin repeated, "The Inner Planets.'' He looked at her and grinned. "It will be like a vacation,'' he said. "By the way, how about my bonus?''

"Bonus?'' Ellen looked puzzled. Then she laughed— but a little strainedly, Templin decided. "Oh, you mean the backing I promised you from Terralune? It's yours, Temp. Ships, and money, and everything you need. Only—'' She hesitated. "That is, I had an idea—''

He interrupted, "That's not what I mean,'' he objected. "My bonus was personnel. You promised me I could have help to settle Venus, if I took care of this mining affair for you. In fact, you said I could take my pick of anybody on the Terralune payroll.''

Ellen's face clouded. "Yes,'' she said. "But, Temp—''

"Don't argue,'' he commanded. "A promise is a promise. And—well, you're on the payroll, Ellen. My advice to you is, start packing. We leave for Venus in the morning!''

Most of my World War II hitch in the Air Force was spent in Italy, and most of the time I played no large part in the war effort. I was a weatherman with a B-24 group on the Foggia plains at first, then a public-relations man for the Twelfth Weather Squadron headquarters. In that capacity I spent as much time as I could in our private rest-and-recreation hotel on the slopes of Mount Vesuvius, the Eremo. "Eremo" is Italian for "hermit," and up there overlooking Capri and the Bay of Naples that's what I was.

Most of Donovan Had a Dream was written there, with an occasional gentle shudder of the ground to remind me where I was, along with the eternal plume from the crater a few thousand feet up the Hill. It was a beautiful place to write, or even just to sit and look out over the vista. It still is. I was there a few years ago with my family, and if I ever have a month to kill in Italy I hope to spend it there. In the early part of 1945, with the war winding down, and my impatience to get back to the real world winding up, it was a lot less attractive to me. Nothing I was doing seemed to be causing the least

*inconvenience to the Japanese or the WEHRMACHT, and
I wanted out.*

*Still, it was, I guess, better than being shot at. And
when duty drove me to the official headquarters in
Caserta, I could always spend time with such boon companions as Eddie Cope, the Sage of Houston, who read
the parts of DONOVAN HAD A DREAM as they came off
the typewriter and offered the wise advice gleaned from
his drama courses at the University of Texas before the
war.*

*I was pretty pleased with DONOVAN HAD A DREAM
when I finished it, still more pleased when THRILLING
WONDER STORIES bought it quickly for more money
than I was used to getting and most pleased of all when I
saw it on the newsstands. They had given it lovely
illustrations by Virgil Finlay. Still better, in an issue that
included Leslie Charteris and many of the best con-
temporary sf writers, lo, "James MacCreigh" led all the
rest. It was the first time I ever received top billing.*

Donovan Had a Dream

1

The Place Called Nard

It was a beautiful city from a distance, the place called Nard. The cloud layer hung a mile overhead and the white towers came almost up to it. You came out of one of the little feeder canals on your canalcraft and there it was, ahead of you. Pure, miraculous white, a city for angels.

"It's the Hags," Hanley said suddenly. "They spoil it."

The narrow-faced man called Valentine stared at him. "Spoil what?" he asked.

"The whole planet." Hanley gestured around him. "Look at this place we're in. A cellar, fixed up with a bar and tables and a couple of dancers who couldn't make a living on Earth. Noise and smoke—dirty glasses with cheap liquor . . ."

Valentine grinned leanly. "That's treason," he commented. "You can't talk about the Hags like that. Besides, it's not their fault."

"No?"

"No. They didn't build this place. They don't make you come here."

"There's no other place to go!"

Valentine shrugged. "Not for the likes of us, no," he admitted. "But there never was a place for men like you and me." He looked around him, at the drunken canalers and their white-faced women. "This is as good a place as any. On Earth there are better places, sure. Cleaner and quieter and the dancers know how to pick up their feet. I've seen them—though you have not. I liked them, but I couldn't stand it for long. That was what they call civilization, Hanley. Civilization means law. Would you like to be law-abiding?"

The broad-shouldered Hanley started, almost spilling his drink in consternation. "Law-abiding? Not me!" he said sincerely.

Valentine nodded and leaned back in his chair. Out in the center of the floor a pair of dancers were going through gymnastic contortions. Silver-haired and slim, the girl spun out of her partner's arms halfway across the floor, stopping near Valentine's table. As she posed there for a second her eyes caught Valentine's gray ones and she gave him the imperceptible performer's smile of greeting. Then the music surged and she spun away.

"Hope Darl didn't hear what you said about dancers." Hanley grinned. "She's smitten."

Valentine picked up his glass and held it to the light. "I wasn't talking about her," he said lazily, watching the milky green opalescent shimmer. "She could do better than this if she wanted to. Don't personalize everything, Hanley."

Hanley pursed his lips, looking at Valentine wonderingly. He too swallowed his drink before he spoke. "How come you live like this, Valentine?" he asked.

"Like what?"

"Like"—Hanley gestured—"like an outlaw. You could be a successful man if you stayed on Earth, Valentine. You talk like a man who's had an education. Yet you hang around this dirty little city on Venus, skirting the edge of the law. It's a good life for me, I guess—I don't know any other. But you . . ."

There was a faraway look in Valentine's brooding

eyes, focused on a table across the smoke-filled room. "Look at that girl," he said suddenly. "The Earthgirl with the Space Fleet ensign."

"The pretty one? What about her?"

"She is pretty, isn't she? But look at her face. You can tell how she has spent her life."

Hanley nodded. "She's been rich—is that what you mean? Rich and powerful. It shows."

"That's what I mean. All her life she's been surrounded by luxury, and she couldn't live for a day if she were alone in the swamps." He set down his glass and faced Hanley. "That's Earth for you," he said. "Soft, and haughty, and weak. Venus is no better, but at least here I can do almost as I like. So I go out into the swamps and bring in bellflowers, and you pass them on to some illegal distillery or other, evading the Hags' tithe, and we both have enough money to do as we please."

Hanley grimaced. "Let's not talk so loud about it," he begged.

The dancers had left the floor and the rickety orchestra was hammering out a dance number. The Earthgirl got up to dance with the youth in Space Fleet blue. Valentine sighed.

"She's still a pretty girl," he said. "Let's have another drink."

"Who's a pretty girl?"

Valentine looked up. The dancer was standing over him, smiling, still wearing the gold-and-scarlet silks of her dancing costume.

"Hello Darl," he said. "I meant you, of course. There isn't a prettier girl in Nard."

A waiter brought a chair over hastily and the girl sank down into it. "You always know the right thing to say," she murmured. "But why didn't you say it to me instead of to Hanley?"

Valentine coughed and detained the waiter. "What would you like?" he asked hurriedly.

She shrugged. "Flower-dew, I suppose. That's what you've been drinking."

Hanley growled, "I'll take whisky. Let's make this one the last, Valentine. We have business."

The waiter vanished and came back with the drinks.

"You needn't be pointed," Darl said. "I can't stay long anyhow. I have to change for my next number. It's something new, Valentine—I wish you could stay and see it."

"Something new?"

"An importation from Earth—an old medieval folk-dance that's being revived. They call it the samba."

"Sounds fascinating," Hanley said. "I'm sorry, but . . ."

"Oh, maybe we can stay," Valentine said. He was looking out over the floor again. "Meanwhile, Darl, let's dance a little. It'll keep you in practice."

"Meaning that I need practice?" she said.

They rose and she walked before him to the floor. The band was still blaring at top speed. They fell into the rhythm of it and moved across the floor.

Darl looked up at him. "Have I told you lately that you missed your vocation?" she asked. "You should have been a dancer. You can dance with me any time. By the way, what *is* your vocation?"

"I'm retired," Valentine said. "Easy . . ." He guided her dextrously among the other couples on the floor. She relaxed against his arm, her eyes half closing.

She felt a nudge from behind and stumbled. Startled, she stared reproachfully up at Valentine.

"I'm sorry," he was saying. "That was clumsy of me."

They had bumped right into another couple—the Earthgirl and the boy in Space Fleet blue. The ensign said, "That's all right," ungraciously, and was about to dance on.

Valentine stopped him. "It was really my fault," he said. "Can we buy you a drink to make up for it?"

The ensign's blond brows lifted. "That's not necessary," he said.

Valentine put a hand on his shoulder. "No, I insist," he said softly.

It was the Earthgirl who spoke. She stood regarding Valentine for a fraction of a second with honest curiosity. Then, "I have a better idea," she said, "let's buy *them* a drink, Van."

The ensign shrugged petulantly. "If you like," he said. To Valentine, "May we?"

"Certainly," Valentine said. The four walked off the floor to the table the Earth couple had occupied. As soon as they had ordered, Valentine said, "I noticed you from across the floor. It's not very often that we see Earthpeople here in Nard."

The ensign permitted himself a smile. "You'll be seeing more of us in the future," he said.

"Really?" Valentine showed genuine interest.

"Sure." The ensign took a deep swallow of his drink. "You'll be seeing more than you ever saw in your life before."

Valentine shook his head gently. "I saw a million and a half Earthmen in the streets of New York, waiting to hear the results of a duel between two professional ray-gun killers," he said.

"Oh, then you've been to Earth," the Earthgirl said. "How did you like it?"

"I admired the beautiful cities, and the immense factories. I didn't think much of the entertainment."

The girl frowned in mock astonishment. "Surely you don't object if two professionals try to kill each other. I understand that all sorts of killing goes on here on Venus. And the people that get killed aren't even being paid for it—it's the Hags killing the Donovans, or the Donovans killing helpless citizens."

"You've been a little misinformed," Valentine said politely. "Is that why you came to Venus? To see some of the killing?"

The ensign laughed explosively. "No. We came on business."

"Mixed with a little pleasure, of course," the girl added swiftly, "In fact, I'm afraid it was almost pleasure. But tell us some more about your reactions to Earth."

They conversed for a few minutes. Valentine con-
scientiously ignored the spectacle of Hanley across the
room, staring incredulously at the foursome. Then Darl
said:

"I've really got to change now. If you'll excuse me
I'll go."

Valentine rose with her and walked as far as the door
to the dressing room, after offering the conventional
thanks for the drink. Then he sat down next to Hanley.

Hanley regarded him with open anger. "What's going
on?" he demanded. "Do you know what time it is?"

Valentine nodded. "Drink your drink, and I'll tell
you all about it."

Hanley grunted and lifted the glass to his lips. He held
it there, then sat bolt upright. "What the heck!" he
murmured. He pointed to the entrance. "Look. What
are *they* doing here?"

Valentine turned around. Every eye in the place was
on the entrance as three new persons came in.

They moved in disdainful silence, like lily-white
swans floating through mire. The first two wore the
white casques of their mysterious order, hiding their
features. The third was a mournful-eyed girl of nineteen
in the scarlet-edged robes of a novice.

"Imagine!" Hanley said. "I never heard of the Hags
coming to a place like this before. Maybe they're human
after all."

"Or maybe they're after something," Valentine said,
his face drawn. "I wish I knew what."

The first Hag threw her casque back, revealing the
lean face of a middle-aged woman. She looked about
her, beckoned imperiously to a waiter in a stained
apron. He approached her uncertainly.

There was a rustle of silken garments behind Valentine, and Darl was back. "Do you see who's here?" she
whispered venomously. "Vultures! I hate those—"

"We all do," Hanley said hastily. He waved at the
dance floor, where the half-intoxicated canalers had
noticed the Hags and were unanimous in their hostile

looks. "I'll bet they haven't got a friend in the place."

The waiter listened uncertainly while the first Hag said something peremptory and short to him, then he hurried off toward a door at one end of the bar. Valentine looked after him thoughtfully.

"Darl," he said without looking at her, "how would you like to do me a favor?"

"Sure."

"Find out what they want."

Darl looked at him uncertainly. She shrugged. "All right." She was on her feet swiftly.

Hanley said, "Valentine, I hate to repeat myself but it's time—"

"I won't be long," he promised. "I'm curious about this."

Darl intercepted the waiter before he reached the door, returned almost immediately. Her eyes were apprehensive.

"They're looking for somebody," she said. "Jay didn't know what they want him for. Valentine, have you been . . ."

Valentine pursed his lips. "Not that I remember," he said.

"Oh, Valentine—don't get into trouble with the Hags. They're *horrible*. They arrested me once. I know what they're like."

Valentine waved his hand. "I won't get into trouble," he said. "Are you ready, Hanley?"

"It's about time," Hanley grumbled. Valentine dropped a bill on the table to cover their drinks, then got up.

"I'll be back, Darl," he promised.

"Tonight?"—eagerly.

"In a couple of days. Good-by."

Valentine noticed the Earthgirl putting on her cloak as he went out. Evidently she was leaving too.

"We're late," Hanley said. "Let's hurry."

The two men walked briskly along the wide street, dimly lighted with luminous disks set in the white-walled buildings. Above, the hanging clouds reflected the more brilliant lights of the center of the city.

"What was it that Darl said about being arrested by the Hags?" Hanley asked.

"It happened a year ago. They picked her up, held her a couple of days, let her go. Never said a word of explanation. She didn't like the Hags much before that—but now she hates them."

They turned into a small street, then into what was almost an alley. They were in the poorer section of Nard now, a place where laborers lived and worked. The buildings were old and small compared with those in the center of the city.

Valentine greeted the man in the black plastic ray-tunic of the police who lounged on the wharf beside his craft, then stepped into it. Hanley followed, with dubious looks at the guard. Ranged against the cushioned seats at the back of the speedbarge were four baled objects—the bellflowers. Their spiced scent was unmistakable. The guard grinned broadly, turned and walked away.

"Here you are," Valentine said. "Now where's your man to take them off my hands?"

"He'll be here," Hanley promised. "Let's get the bales up on the wharf if you're sure it's safe."

"Safe as the secrets of the Donovans," Valentine said. "Even the Hags can't find those out."

The two men worked quickly and in moments the bales were stacked beside the boat. They climbed out. Hanley plucked a bellflower petal out of a bale and chewed it reflectively.

"Look over there," he said, pointing. "What do you make of that?"

Valentine looked. "What?" A low-wheeled car purred down toward them along the canal street, stopped at a shabby building not far away. Two persons got out, a man and a girl. At that distance it was hard to identify them but the man was in blue uniform.

"Our friends from the cafe!" Valentine said. "Wonder what they're doing here? That's—oh, I understand. See the Earthsign?"

Hanley nodded as his eyes took in the two interlocked squares that gleamed faintly over the entrance to the building.

"An Earth storehouse, huh? I can see why the boy wonder would be down here—in charge of a shipment, maybe. But how about the girl?"

Valentine shrugged. "It doesn't make sense to me either," he conceded. "But these Earthgirls—oh, here comes your man."

2

Man Meets Donovan

A short man was walking rapidly toward them, his face tense. As soon as he got within earshot: "Sorry I'm late," he said. "I had a little trouble." He was obviously uneasy, eyes squinted and blinking.

"What kind of trouble?"

The man spat expressively. "The Hags," he said. "I don't know how much longer this little deal of ours is going to work. I've got an uneasy feeling. The Hags are searching for the still."

"Searching?" Hanley repeated. "That's bad. Will they find it?"

"Not unless they look somewhere else." The man sighed and regarded the bales meditatively. "They were looking in my house. I'm not crazy enough to keep the still there. But it looks like they've got a line on me."

Valentine nodded. "Well, do you want to take this batch?"

The man spread his hands morosely. "I have to," he said. "My customers are waiting." He widened a gap in the sacking of the bales, peered at the exposed bellflowers. "Looks all right. Wait just a minute."

He turned his back and walked across the street to where a light cargo car was parked, drove it over to them. The three men together heaved the bales into its cargo space.

They had just finished when the short man froze. "Watch out," he whispered. "Look who's coming."

Valentine gave him a quick glance, then relaxed. "Oh, the policeman," he said. "Don't worry about him. He's a friend of mine—I pay him more than the Hags do." But the guard seemed anxious as he approached.

He said, "I thought I'd better tell you. There's a robot coming this way. It just came over the talker." He patted the portable two-way radio he carried.

"A robot?" Hanley grunted.

"Yeah. Coming fast."

Hanley's business associate gurgled in his throat.

"They're out for blood," he said. He stood there uncertainly. "I've got the stuff already. I might as well stay with it." He shrugged and his hand went into his pocket for a wad of colored paper, which he gave to Hanley. "I'll let you know later if I'm still in business," he said. He got into the cargo car and was gone.

Hanley looked after him. "Well, what now?" he asked.

"I don't know," Valentine admitted. "Maybe you and I will have to find a legal way of making a living after all." His eyes strayed past Hanley, looking down the street. "We're stuck—look."

Hanley turned and followed his glance. "It wasn't a false alarm, was it?"

Far down the street, beyond the worried back of the guard, a figure was approaching rapidly. It was large, menacing—and not even remotely human.

The serf-robots of the Hags were huge creatures —round-bodied, capped at the shoulders with a many-eyed dome, borne upon a pair of stiltlike metal legs. They had no intelligence in the sense that a man is intelligent but they could respond instantly to radio-control from afar, and what they saw and heard was transmitted to the person controlling them.

The policeman, now a hundred yards away, turned and gave them a fleeting look of warning. Valentine nodded.

Hanley asked apprehensively: "Do you think it's after us?"

"I don't know," Valentine said. "We'll find out."

The creature bore down upon them, then halted in the middle of the street. It seemed to listen to an inaudible order, then whirled and dashed into one of the buildings.

"It wasn't looking for us, then," Hanley observed with heartfelt relief. "Well, thank heaven for that."

Valentine was frowning. "Now I wonder what it *was* after."

"Bellflower smugglers like us. That's what the guard—"

Valentine snorted. "In there? That's an Earth depot."

Hanley grunted staring. It had been the Earth-marked warehouse into which the robot had dashed.

"Well, I guess not. Say! The car's gone. Our friend must have left."

"I noticed that. Wish I knew what was going on."

"It's no business of ours," Hanley protested. "Let's go."

"All right. Go ahead, Hanley. I'll see you later. I'm going to find out what that robot's after."

"What do you care? You're just looking for trouble." The puzzled, half-comprehending look was in Hanley's eyes again.

"I do care, though," Valentine said. "That's what matters right now. Go ahead—travel."

Valentine waited a half second after Hanley had melted into the shadows of the goods piled on the other side of the street. He ran lightly across the street, down toward the Earth warehouse. He paused in the doorway to make sure no one was watching, then silently slipped inside.

He was in a dusty office with covered writing machines and desks, completely deserted. Valentine heard no sound anywhere. He blinked, then walked softly across the small room to a gaping double door.

Inside was impenetrable blackness, a large storeroom of some kind. Valentine could sense, rather than see, metal crates stacked along the wall by his side. A heap of them before him blocked his vision.

He stood silent, trying to match the super-sensitive hearing of the robot with his own forest-trained ears. Far off there was a faint scratching sound. He stepped soundlessly forward—and slipped, flailed the air wildly to regain his balance, stood teetering for a second. Something was there on the floor that was liquid and slippery.

His nostrils explained it to him even before he carefully bent down, reached out exploring hands. His fingers touched something warm and solid—a human body! The reek of human blood flowed around him. Valentine pursed his lips and rose to his feet. He could do no good for the man—and the body was a fresh warning of what his own fate might be.

More cautiously he tiptoed forward. As he neared the end of the stack of crates he detached a faint vertical line of light before him. He peered round the boxes, ready to race for safety at an instant's warning.

Far down the long aisle of crates towered the bulk of the robot. A thin beam of light blazed from a socket in the creature's domed top, flared down on an eight-foot crate held effortlessly in the great tentacles. As Valentine watched, the robot set the crate down, reached for another and examined it.

The electric scanners that were its eyes took seconds to grasp the stenciled characters on the box, even with the aid of the light. Valentine wondered whether, somewhere in the brooding city, a Hag sat watching a telescreen reflecting the things the robot saw, or whether it was on its memory tape alone that the image was recorded.

From behind him there came a crash.

Valentine whirled, his eyes staring into blackness. There was a scrambling noise, then silence. But the robot had heard too! The floor-jolting strides of its massive feet jarred him into action.

His mind raced desperately. Better to face the unknown danger behind him than the sure annihilation by the robot! He darted back around the crates, stumbling crazily in the blackness. He plunged into the office, reckless of the danger. Amazingly, it was empty! And the wide door to the empty bright street stood open.

But he slid to a halt on impulse. He dodged toward the corner of the office and slipped under a desk. The robot would be sure to catch him in straight pursuit in the street. But if he remained hidden and very quiet . . .

Clattering like a boiler-factory on the run, the robot pounded through the office. Only a single cursory sweep of its search-beam it gave to the office before it hurtled on through the door. It paused irresolutely outside. Then its earphones picked up the footsteps of some luckless pedestrian and it was off in a mechanical rush in pursuit.

Valentine came cautiously out from under the desk, listening. If the monster's search carried it far enough away it would be possible to escape. Otherwise . . .

"Valentine!"

The voice was a whisper, from the open door to the storeroom.

"Hanley!" Valentine gasped in recognition. "I thought you . . ."

"I know what you thought," Hanley said apologetically. "Are there any more robots around?"

"I don't think so. What are you doing here?"

There was a repetition of the scrambling noise.

Valentine, coming nearer, knew that Hanley was climbing down from the top of the heap of crates.

"I thought it was safer up there after I tripped," he excused himself. "I guess I messed things up, huh? I thought you might need some help, so I followed you.

Then I stumbled over this kid here, and when I got up I knocked one of these crates over.''

"You stumbled over the dead man?"

"Dead? No—I listened, and heard the heartbeat. Look, Valentine, let's get her out of here. She's not dead—and she's not a man!''

The dark clouds overhead were beginning to grow light with dawn as they pushed the canalcraft away from the jetty, sent it slicing the unrippled surface of the water and out into the middle of the canal.

"Where to?" Hanley asked from the wheel. "My place down at the edge of the city?"

"We'll go there first," Valentine said. "I'll drop you off there but the girl and I are going on. I've got a plan for her.''

He ignored Hanley's questioning eyes and turned to the girl. He had recognized her instantly as the Earthgirl from the canalers' cafe.

Obviously, she had been knocked out by the great tantacles of the robot. Skin was ripped from her arms, a bloody welt marked the hairline at one side of her face. She had lost much blood.

Hanley had been gentle as he carried her in his powerful arms and the blood had clotted to flow no longer.

"Hand me the kit from the locker," Valentine said. He raised her head, propped it up. With the material in the medical kit he dressed her wounds as best he could. He took out a slim hypodermic, slipped an ampoule of colorless fluid into the barrel, worked the plunger to puncture the capsule. Then he inserted it carefully into the blue-traced vein at the inside of the girl's elbow, pressed down the plunger. The girl twitched and moaned.

"What's that?" Hanley called from the wheel.

"I'm giving her a shot of nihilate to keep her asleep. She'll be a lot less trouble that way.''

Hanley frowned. "Listen, Valentine—you can trust me. Where are you going to take her?"

Valentine hesitated, watching the girl. The expression on her face faded into the relaxed mask of slumber as the drug took effect.

He rose to face Hanley. "Maybe you'd better not know," he said. "I trust you. But maybe you'd better do your own guessing."

Hanley shrugged and faced forward. The speedy barge had almost reached the limits of the city. Valentine came forward to take the wheel as Hanley turned it in toward the shore.

"I'll see you in a few days," he promised. "Sorry, but this is important."

"Sure," Hanley said morosely. He relinquished the wheel. Then, "Hold it!" he said sharply. "Look what's waiting for us!"

Valentine's eyes flew to the dock before him.

Standing silent and watchful at the corner of the street which led to Hanley's home was one of the robots of the Hags!

The barge spun around in a sharp turn and Valentine thrust the speed lever forward to the last notch.

"That settles it," he said. "He may have seen the girl. We can't land."

"He might just be standing there," Hanley offered.

"And he might not, too. They could have traced the bellflowers to you—anything. We can't take the chance. I'm sorry, Hanley, but I think you'll have to come along with us now."

"And where are we going?" Hanley asked.

Valentine looked at him with a faint smile. "I think you have a pretty good idea. Why don't you try a guess?"

Hanley nodded slowly and the half-understanding that had been in his eyes became certainty.

"It's the Donovans," he whispered. "You're one of the Donovans, aren't you?"

Valentine nodded and Hanley was silent for several seconds.

"I've been having that idea in the back of my head

for a long time," Hanley said. "It's the only thing that made sense. But . . ."

"But what?"

Hanley coughed. "Well, I thought the Donovans were a pretty rough lot. Outside of being pirates, I mean. Of course, all I know about the Donovans is what I heard from the Hags—mind you, I'm not saying they're right . . ."

Valentine shrugged. "We're not even pirates," he said. "Oh, we *have* stopped freight barges once in a while when there was something on them we had to have. But we only stole from the Hags—and they stole the whole planet of Venus from the people."

"But I thought the Hags always flew."

"They do now." Valentine laughed. "We taught them that."

Hanley nodded. "But how did you get along?"

"Well—did you ever wonder what I did with the money you gave me for bellflowers? We bought a lot of things, and made a lot. We have factories. Everything we ever stole was something the Hags had that we couldn't get any other way. Stuff from their laboratories mostly."

"I had an idea that the Hags exaggerated a little," Hanley admitted. "Well, anything they say is probably a lie, of course. But why do you live in caves in the swamp, like animals?"

Valentine laughed shortly. "You'll see," he promised.

"Oh." Hanley grimaced. "Then I'm going to the Donovan hideout."

"I'm afraid you'll have to. Don't feel badly about it—it's an honor. Only the Donovans have ever been there before."

"And the girl?"

Valentine shrugged, and dropped the conversation.

He turned to look behind him. The Hags had fast canalcraft too, of course, and there was always the possibility of chase. But he saw nothing.

The canal, at this hour of the morning, was deserted.

The girl moaned in her sleep. Valentine sighed and leaned back, holding the wheel loosely.

3

Every Word a Lie

After miles of the straightaway, the canal's course took a wide turn and the white spires of Nard disappeared behind the dense trees. Valentine stretched, sat upright, began to pay attention to the shoreline. His gray eyes roved along the tangled vegetation of the bank. After a moment he changed course slightly, ran the canalcraft in toward the shore in a long slant. Where a bent tangletree hung its weeping fronds far out over the water he cast a quick look behind him, then gave the craft hard right tiller.

"What—" Hanley gasped. Then he understood, as the drooping fronds brushed the top of the craft and he could see behind their screen.

It was another waterway, a hidden one. Apparently it had once been a natural shallow stream, for its course was winding. But it was deep enough for the shallow draft of a canalcraft and careful work had cleared enough of the vegetation to make it navigable without destroying the overhead screen.

"Clever," Hanley said. "And you have your huts under the trees, huh? Moving around from time to time so the Hags won't find you?''

Valentine smiled. "We don't move very often," he said. "This is the original Donovan hideout. It's been here a hundred and fifty years, ever since old Donovan himself took his followers out of the cities."

After a winding, mile-long run under the shrouding trees they drew up to a metal landing stage. Half a dozen canalcraft were moored there already, slim shapes that indicated speed.

Valentine stepped out and raised his hands. "Valentine of the Donovans," he said to an unseen listener. "I have two strangers. I bind myself for them."

There was a rustling in the undergrowth and a man in jungle green stepped out, putting a ray-pencil into its sheath. He stared at Hanley and the girl doubtfully.

"Go ahead, Valentine," he said. "I guess you know what you are doing."

Valentine nodded and beckoned to Hanley, who handed the girl out to him, then stepped onto the stage himself.

"Lead on," Hanley said. "Here—I'll carry the girl."

She was light enough but Valentine relinquished the chore of carrying her to Hanley's great strength.

"This way," he said, and set off on a narrow path.

Hanley looked about curiously for the huts or caves he had expected. He could see nothing, nothing but the thick trees and tangled creepers that writhed along the ground.

"Here we are," Valentine said. A huge boulder stood beside the path before them. Hanley watched in astonishment as Valentine stood before it.

"Who is it?" a voice asked, Hanley couldn't locate the voice's owner—a hidden microphone, he thought.

Valentine repeated what he had said to the guard at the landing stage. There was a slight electric drone, and the face of the rock opened up before him. Within was a broad, shallow flight of steps going down. Another guard with a ray-rod stood inside the entrance, his hand on a lever.

"Come ahead," he said.

Valentine looked around at Hanley and grinned. "This is our hideout," he said. "Welcome to the Donovan caves!"

The whispered buzz of an interphone awakened Donovan. He was at once alert, though he had slept for less than three hours. He flipped a switch beside his bed and spoke.

A voice replied, "This is Surgeon-of-the-day Carla. I promised I'd call when your Earthgirl was able to talk. Well, she's ready whenever you want her."

"Good," said Valentine. "I'll be right down."

He stepped into a tingling shower and quickly dressed. Just outside his room was a small chamber where a man was seated at a table, idly reading.

"Hello, Valentine," he said. "I sent for some food for you." He gestured toward a group of covered vessels on the table before him.

Valentine nodded and sat down. A tap on the covers of the vessels made them hiss satisfyingly. Then Valentine lifted the lids off easily, revealing food kept warm by units in the lids, kept from spoilage by the vacuum. Pouring a cup of the pale, effervescent liquid, he nodded at the door next to his own.

"Hanley isn't awake yet?"

The guard shook his head. "What shall I do with him when he comes out?" he asked.

"Feed him first, I suppose. After that—well, he'll probably be asking a lot of questions. He was pretty surprised at finding a city as big as this underground. Tell him whatever he wants to know."

"Anything?" The guard raised his brows.

"That's right. He knows too much now if we can't trust him. A little more won't make any difference." Valentine chuckled. "You'd better brace yourself for a hard time. I could hardly get him to go to sleep when we came in—he had an idea we were savages, living in caves."

He quickly finished eating, then walked through broad bright corridors to what a plaque identified as the medical section.

"Hello, Carla," he said to the surgeon of the day. "How's the girl?"

Carla was a slim young man in a white tunic. He hesitated. "She's only had a couple of hours under the vita-rays. Actually it would be better if we kept her there. She's lost a lot of blood."

"You can put her under again afterward, Carla. This is important."

Carla shrugged. "All right. She's well enough to talk now. But try not to get her too excited." He led the way out of the room.

The girl was supine on a dais, under gleaming orange lights. They peered in at her through the crystal wall of the chamber in which she lay. Carla touched a switch outside the entrance and the lights flicked and blanched to normal daylight color. He opened the door and motioned Valentine in ahead of him.

The blood had been washed from her and her cuts had closed. Carla thumbed down a lower eyelid and peered at the pupil. Satisfied, he took a small plastic capsule from a pouch at his waist and expertly crushed it in his fingers, close to the girl's nostrils. A sharp, tingling pungency filled the room. The girl shuddered and almost immediately awoke.

Paying no attention to her, Carla turned to Valentine.

"She'll be all right for a while. Call me when you leave and I'll put her back under the rays."

There was surprise and fear in almost equal proportions in the girl's eyes. Valentine said, "Probably you're wondering where you are."

The girl frowned at him. "You—you're the man who bumped into us in the cafe."

"Yes. My name is Valentine. You were injured last night by a serf-robot belonging to the Hags—do you remember? I found you and brought you here."

The girl pushed herself erect, sat with her legs

dangling over the side of the pallet. She regarded him carefully.

"Where is 'here'?" she asked. Valentine noticed again that her voice was exceptionally rich and deep. She was attractive enough, he thought. If her skin hadn't been just a trifle too dark, in spite of the bleaching effect of the vita-rays, she might have been almost beautiful.

He asked, "Have you ever heard of the Donovans?"

"Donovans? Yes, surely. They're the outlaws. The savages who live in huts in the jungle."

Valentine smiled ruefully. "It seems to me I've heard that too many times today," he said. "We're not exactly savages. You see, I'm one of the Donovans. This place you're in now is our jungle city."

Her lips parted. "Oh? But I thought—that is, all the Venusians said that—"

"I know what they said," Valentine interrupted. "They said we were outlaws. They're partly right."

The girl nodded hesitantly. Then, remembering, she flexed her arm experimentally. She rubbed it, looked at it. The cuts where the robot had flailed it had closed, leaving only pinkish welts under the regenerative influence of the vita-rays.

"You're quite civilized," she admitted. "I shouldn't have expected vita-rays. I suppose I owe you something for helping me. I'll see that my father rewards you."

Valentine coughed. "That brings up a delicate point. I'm afraid we'll have to keep you here for some time."

"Keep me?" The warmth had gone from her voice.

"Yes. You see, our safety would be endangered if the Hags knew as much about us as you do."

"But what has that to do with me? I'm not a Venusian. I have credentials from the Earth government—a trade mission."

Valentine shook his head impatiently. "Credentials from Earth are worthless here," he said. "The Earth government doesn't even know we exist."

* * *

The girl slipped to her feet, eyes bright and fixed on Valentine's. "I'm Elena Orris," she said softly. "My father is an important man." She examined Valentine's face closely, with obvious vexation that the name made no impression on him. "Do you know what that means?"

"What does it mean?"

"It means that my father can call out the Earth-fleet if you hold me here. The whole fleet—eight thousand battle rockets. Do you know what battle rockets could do to you?"

Donovan said patiently, "You don't understand. The fleet could blast us to shreds, yes. But how would they ever find us? The Hags can't find us, and they've been looking for over a century. As far as anyone on Earth would ever know, you mysteriously disappeared. The Hags won't press the investigation too far. After all, it was their robot that attacked you. They can't be sure you're still alive."

The girl bit her lip and looked at him uncertainly. Then, "Tell me what you want," she said.

"That's better," Valentine applauded. He sat down facing her. "There are some questions I want to ask you. About those crates in the storeroom the robot was so interested in. What was in them?"

"I can't tell you."

"Why?"

Elena Orris hesitated. "I—I can't. I swore an oath. I'm not here as a tourist, you know. This is part of my job. The Earth government sent me to make sure that the goods got here safely. It's important that it be kept a secret."

"It's important to me, too. Who was it for?"

She shrugged. "A man named—Smith. I don't know him."

"Do you know who he's acting for?"

"No."

Valentine stood up, took a step toward her. "I tell you, we Donovans have got to know all about this," he

said. "We're not savages. We don't usually force people
to talk. But this is different."

The girl gasped. "Are you threatening me?"

"With torture? No. With being made to answer,
yes."

"You can't make me answer!"

Valentine smiled humorlessly. "We can try. There's a
sort of hypnosis technique we've worked out. It's very
good."

"I'll never submit to it!"

"It's not up to you," Valentine explained. "There's a
drug that goes with it so that your cooperation isn't
necessary. Unfortunately, it sometimes affects the
mind."

The girl winced. "Beast!" she whispered. "I'll tell
you."

"Thank you," Valentine said gravely. "What was in
the cases?"

In a dull tone she said, "Atomic explosives. Uranium
isotopes and the catalyst to make them work."

Valentine frowned thoughtfully. "What about this
man Smith?"

"I don't know much about him. He came to my
father on Earth—my father is the Industries Controller
for the Earth government. Smith wanted what he called
industrial explosives. He offered money and concessions on Venus."

"Strange the Hags couldn't make their own uranium
isotopes," Valentine observed. "Venus has plenty of
carnotite. I thought I knew all the Venusian officials
that work for the Hags but I never heard of Smith."

"It may not have been his real name. But his credentials were good. My father investigated."

"Of course, there's something else about it that's
peculiar, you realize. The Hags are the government of
Venus. Why would they send one of their robots to pry
into something that they themselves had bought and
paid for?"

She shrugged. "You know as much as I do. Ensign
Drake brought me down to look the shipment over

before I went to bed. The guard on duty—an Earth-man—complained of some kind of a fever and asked to be relieved. Ensign Drake took him to his quarters to get another man, and I stayed behind to keep an eye on the place. We didn't expect any trouble. I was just waiting for him when—when that robot came blundering in." She shuddered. "I don't think it really meant any harm—not unless I got in its way. It just sort of pushed me aside."

Valentine looked at her thoughtfully, then at his watch. "I must go," he said. "I'll be back. Until then, the surgeon says you'll be better off under the vita-rays. You can do as you like—except that you can't leave."

He left her staring after him. On the way out he stopped to talk to the medic.

"See that she's fed and kept out of trouble," he said. "I'll be back."

"I'll put her to sleep and give her some more rays," Carla promised. "Did she tell you what you wanted to know?"

Valentine grimaced. "She wouldn't tell me a thing at first. I had to threaten to use force on her finally."

"And then—did she talk?"

"She talked." Valentine smiled humorlessly. "She answered every question—and every word she spoke was a lie!"

4

Alliance Refused

Valentine switched the teletalker in his room to *Record* and dictated a full account of what he had seen for the benefit of the council of the Donovans. As he was finishing the story he heard voices outside the door and Hanley came in.

"You've got a wonderful place here, Valentine," he said enthusiastically. "I'm sorry about—you know, about what I said about caves."

"Sure," Valentine said absentmindedly.

"That guy who was outside took me for a walk around. This place is immense—eleven thousand people, he told me. Growing your own food, operating your own factories, everything underground. Wonderful!"

Valentine smiled. "I suppose you know all our secrets now," he said.

Hanley looked embarrassed. "Yeah, I guess so. Look, Valentine. That's something I wanted to talk to you about. Understand, I don't care if I ever go back to Nard—I like it here. But if I do go back I want you to know I won't say a word to anybody."

"We'll be sure of that," Valentine said ambiguously. "Did your escort tell you everything you wanted to know about us?" He sat down and lit a greenish cigarette.

"Well, almost. But there are one or two things. For instance, who runs this place? How did it get started?"

Valentine pursed his lips and blew a long plume of smoke.

"It goes back over a hundred and fifty years," he said. "The Hags rewrote the histories, so you probably don't know much about it. But back in two thousand one hundred and sixty-nine Venus was a colony belonging to Earth."

"Oh, sure. I knew that."

Valentine nodded. "And the Hags were a brand-new order on Earth. They had just begun operating, oh maybe ten or fifteen years before. They were a sort of a crazy imitation of a religious order—composed of women who thought that men had made a mess of the world. They were brilliant women, of course. Doctors, chemists, physicists—everything."

"Then what?"

"Then they got into trouble." Valentine frowned thoughtfully. "Even we Donovans don't know exactly what they did. I was curious about it when I was going to college on Earth—a lot of us go to Earth for schooling—so I looked in the old records. But all I could find were hints. I think they began using men in biological experiments. And somehow word of it got out, and they were banished from Earth. And they came here."

"To Venus? The government let them come?"

"There was no other place for them. They started a revolution, persuading the colonials that they had been unjustly banished and they could give them democracy and freedom."

"That's a laugh."

"Yes, but it sounded better in those days. There was a lot of justice in what they told the people. Earth had been pretty grasping, looting Venus without compunction. So the people fought their revolution for them and Earth didn't have as big a space fleet as it has now and we won. That is—the Hags won. The people, of course, were no better off than they had been. Maybe worse.''

Hanley shifted uncomfortably. ''Sure,'' he said. ''That's very interesting. But how about the Donovans? Where'd they come from?''

Valentine stood up. ''Let's take a walk around while we're talking,'' he said. ''You can't have seen the whole city.''

''Sure,'' Hanley said, rising and following him through the door. They walked down a broad, brilliantly lighted corridor toward a large chamber where many people were moving about. ''You were telling me where the Donovans came from,'' he reminded.

''There was a man named Jeremiah Donovan,'' Valentine said. ''He was one of the leaders in the rebellion. He preached democracy to the people and they followed him. When the revolution was won he began trying to put democracy into practice and the Hags arrested him as a traitor.''

''How do you like that? After he fought for them.''

''He escaped, though. He tried to fight the Hags. It was a good fight but they had everything on their side. About a hundred and fifty men were left after a month of it and they followed Donovan out into the swamps. They built this city—or began it, anyhow. At first the story about the caves was true.''

Hanley nodded and stared about him. They were in an immense underground chamber. A deep pool of crystalline water was at one end of it and men and women were swimming or lounging about under the bright sunlamps on the dome forty feet overhead. Others were moving about purposefully from corridors opening into the chamber to boothlike affairs in the chamber itself.

Hanley said, ''With all these people, why can't you come out into the open? You must outnumber the Hags.''

"But they have robots," Valentine explained. "We don't."

"Can't you make them?"

"We're trying. But we aren't having much success because we can't duplicate the alloy the Hags use in the electronic brains. Duplicate it? We don't even know what it is!"

"Can't you—well, capture one?"

"We have. In fact"—he hesitated—"in fact, we've captured several different types."

"Different types? But I've only seen one kind."

Valentine nodded. "I think the others are experimental. One was built into an aircraft that crashed. It ran the plane. And on the same ship were three or four *little* ones. Really little—about the size of a pinhead."

Hanley whistled. "Wonder what they were for."

Valentine said wryly. "So do we. We've taken them apart and analyzed them and we still don't know what we've got. They were just the brains of the robot—the radio cell that controls it."

They sat down on a broad bench next to the pool. Valentine stared into the water thoughtfully.

Hanley said, "How come you know so much about the Hags?"

"Oh, various ways. We monitor their radio—hear everything they broadcast. And we keep a couple of men close to their palace in Nard. But they're smart too and we don't find out as much as we'd like to."

"Oh." Hanley fell silent for a moment, watching the people of the underground city. "What's that place over there, where all the people are coming and going?"

Valentine looked. "That's the Council Hall. The government of the city is handled there. By the Council of the Donovans. I'm a member of the Council. There are thirty-five of us." He smiled ruefully. "By rights I should be in there now, answering questions for them."

"What questions?"

"Questions about the Earthgirl. But I don't know the

answers to them. Questions like what is she doing on Venus, and what is in those crates, and—''

Hanley interrupted by snapping his fingers. ''Me and my memory,'' he grunted. ''I knew there was something I wanted to tell you. He fished in a pocket, pulled out a couple of flat silvery disks and handed them to Valentine.

''What are these?'' Valentine asked, fingering them curiously.

Hanley grinned. ''While I was up on the crates—remember?—I knocked one over and broke it open. It spilled all over. I picked these things up. The crates were full of them.''

When Valentine walked in Elena was sitting on the dais in the crystal room, furiously smoking a cigarette. As soon as she saw him she burst out:

''I'm going insane! Why don't you let me out of here? I've told you what you wanted. Now keep your end of the bargain. Let me go!''

Valentine looked at her coldly for a second.

''We made no bargain. And if we had you didn't keep it.''

''I didn't keep it?''

''Yes. I asked you what was in those crates.''

Elena Orris opened her eyes wide. ''Of course. I told you—they're supposed to contain industrial explosives. My father's men inspected them just before we left.''

Valentine laughed aloud. ''You're magnificent,'' he said. Then, opening his hand to display what he held: ''Look. Is this your industrial explosive?''

The girl stared at the disk incredulously. ''You—but where—'' Abruptly the strength seemed to flow out of her. She looked up at Valentine helplessly.

Valentine sat down facing her. ''Start telling me the truth now,'' he ordered. ''The real truth—bearing in mind that twenty minutes ago this thing was in several pieces and one of our radio techs was telling me all he could about it. Or do we have to use the drug?''

Elena said sullenly, ''I'm not a radio tech. I don't

know very much about them."

"Tell me as much as you do know. Who were they for?"

She said, "They are for—for the Earthmen on Venus."

"Earthmen?"

"Yes. The Embassy staff. Commercial missions. Every Earthman on Venus—almost a thousand of them. Most of them right in Nard."

Valentine frowned. "And what are the Earthmen going to do with them?"

"That's the part I don't know," Elena said flatly. "They—they had something to do with robots."

"With the Hags' robots?" Valentine's face was impassive but his mind was racing. "You mean with the radio-control of the robots? Some radio device . . .?"

"I think so. I think these things interfere with the radio-waves between the robots and wherever they're controlled from. I heard my father talking about them once. He called them 'wavetraps'. They just sort of reach out and *absorb* radio waves."

Valentine said slowly, "And that would mean that the robots would be helpless. They'd be blind, deaf and paralyzed." He took that thought in silently, liking it, hardly daring to believe it. So powerful a weapon . . . "What were you supposed to do with these things?" he asked.

"Just bring them here. Ensign Drake was actually in charge of them but I was sent along to watch Ensign Drake. He was going to turn them over to the Embassy staff tomorrow."

Valentine stared at her curiously. "That doesn't strike you as being unethical?" he asked. "To just attack like that?"

"Unethical?" she echoed. "Are the Hags ethical?"

"You have a point," he admitted. He turned the idea over in his mind. Mechanisms to paralyze the robots, meant for the Earth Colony on Venus. An Earth plot—a plan to wrest the planet away from the Hags, make it again a colony of Terra!

He looked soberly at the girl. Absently he noticed that she was strangely pale—then he remembered she had been under the vita-rays. Life moved faster under the vita-rays. Without compensating ultra-violet, her newly regenerated skin was pale, bleaching as much in a few hours as it might otherwise have done in months.

She watched him uncertainly. Then her expression changed as a new thought crossed her mind. "Valentine!" she said eagerly. "I have an idea! You hate the Hags, don't you?"

He laughed. "I couldn't love them."

"We hate them too! Oh, Valentine, why can't we join forces? As allies we couldn't lose!"

"Allies? The Earth government—and we outlaws?"

"Certainly! Earth would help you. With our Space Fleet, our weapons, you could destroy the Hags in a few days. They could be wiped out completely—and you could come out of hiding."

Valentine listened without changing expression. He said, "And what would happen after that? What does Earth want from Venus?"

Elena Orris spread her hands. "Only friendship," she said persuasively. "Friendship and trade. Venus has millions of tons of radioactive ore—I'll be truthful with you, Valentine. We need it. Our mines are running low."

"Can't you get it from the Hags without overthrowing them?"

"We've tried. They won't listen to reason. Undeveloped resources that mean life to Earth—and the Hags won't let us develop them. That's all we want. Nothing that will hurt Venus, just—"

"Just the chance to make it a colony again," Valentine finished for her. "You used the wrong word. You don't want allies—you want slaves!"

5

Escape

Elena recoiled from him, anger in her eyes. She whispered, "Don't forget, swamp-dweller, Earth can *take* what it needs! Help us and we'll reward you. Try to stop us and you'll be exterminated along with the Hags!"

Valentine nodded his head unwillingly. He admitted, "Unfortunately there's some truth in what you say. If you can stop the robots you can take over the planet—and Earth will be more dangerous than the Hags to us."

"Well? Why not accept my proposition?"

Valentine said patiently, "For two reasons. First, I can't speak for all the Donovans and you can't speak for Earth. Second, I'm not sure you can stop the robots."

"Don't worry about it," Elena boasted. "The wave-traps work. The Hags have only one type of robot—we know that. We tried it out. It stopped the robot cold."

"Oh." Valentine studied her thoughtfully. "Are you sure that the Hags only have the one type?"

"Positive! We've had reports from agents in the Hag Palace itself."

Valentine nodded noncommittally and stood up. "Well, there's only one thing to do," he said. "I'll report what you say to the Council of the Donovans. If they agree I'll come and tell you." He nodded a farewell and turned toward the door.

"Wait!" Elena Orris sprang after him. "Don't leave me in this jail! I hate it!"

Valentine looked at her in surprise. "Where do you want to go?"

"Back to Nard! You can see why I must. That robot was prying into the crates. I want to find out what he discovered."

Valentine shook his head. "You're being absurd. Obviously we can't let you go. No one but the Donovans knows about this place and we can't take a chance that you might tell the Hags about it."

"Good heavens!" She stamped her foot in anger. "Are you deaf, Valentine? I told you that you and I would fight the Hags together. Why would I turn you over to them when I need your help?"

"Oh, you might find some reason," Valentine said. "No, you'll have to stay here for a while. Later on we'll see."

Hanley was open-mouthed when Valentine switched off the recorder and turned to him. "Was all that stuff true?" he asked. "Are the Earthies planning to take us over?"

Valentine grinned. "The Earthgirl said it. I think this time she was telling the truth."

"Well, what are we going to do about it? They'd be as bad as the Hags."

"Worse," Valentine admitted. "I don't know what we'll do. The Council of the Donovans will have to decide. They'll report in a few hours. Meanwhile . . ."

"Yeah?"

"Meanwhile you and I can take another look around Nard." He scrutinized Hanley's face carefully. Slowly,

"You see, I'm taking your word that you're on our side now."

"Oh, I won't spill anything, Valentine."

"I know you won't. And anyhow I have to take the chance."

"What are we going to do in Nard?"

"Look around. We'll take up where we left off last night."

Hanley grimaced. "I hope the Hags don't remember what we look like," he said. "Suppose they've still got a robot in the depot?"

"That's what we have to find out. The crates are important. If the Hags have a good look at them, they know something is up. And I'm afraid they've had their chance.

"I'm with you," Hanley said. "I don't see much future in it, though. If the Hags see us poking around in a thing like that . . ."

The interphone buzzed sharply, interrupting him. Valentine flicked the switch on. "Go ahead."

"Valentine!" a voice crackled. "This is the guard post at Main Gate. The Earthgirl has knocked out the guard here and got away."

Valentine looked over the shoulder of the medico who was working on the guard. "What was it?" he asked.

"Some kind of a drug. I'll have him around in a minute."

The guard commander said, "There are five men out patroling for her. She can't get very far."

"How did she get up here in the first place?" Valentine asked him.

"Carla called from the surgery a minute ago. One of his men found him unconscious. When they woke him up he said he was all set to put her to sleep but she snatched the nihilate needle out of his hand. That's all he remembers."

"She must have done the same thing to the guard," Valentine conjectured, his brows drawn. He turned to

look at the guard, who was stirring, shaking his head.
He opened his eyes.

"That girl! She stabbed me," he said.

"With a nihilate needle," Valentine said. "How did it
happen? Weren't you on the watch for the Earthgirl?"

"Earthgirl?" the guard repeated. "She didn't look
like an Earthie. She wasn't dark, and there wasn't
anything about her clothes . . ."

"The vita-rays," Valentine said. "They bleached her.
Well, it doesn't matter. What did she do?"

The guard shakily stood up. He said, "She just came
up to me without saying anything. I was going to ask her
what she wanted, when I saw something shiny in her
hand, and—"

The guard officer interrupted them. "Here comes
that patrol," he said. As soon as they were close
enough, "Where's the girl?"

"She's gone," the first man panted. "Fenwick and
Cavally are chasing her. She took one of the barges at
the stage."

Valentine paused no longer. "Come on!" he yelled to
Hanley. "We'll follow her. There's still a chance."

He dashed down the short jungle path to the landing
stage in the hidden canal. No longer were there several
neat silvery barges tied up at the side. There were only
two and they were adrift. Obviously the girl had stolen
one for her escape, cut the others loose. And by the
stage, with the fifth man of the patrol bending over him,
lay the figure of yet another guard.

"She doesn't care *who* she stabs," Hanley grunted.
"Hey, what are you doing?"

Without wasting time Valentine leaped far out over
the water into the nearest of the idly floating canalcraft.
The vessel bobbed and rocked dangerously under the
impact of his weight, but didn't capsize. He quickly
seized the controls, started the motor, headed back
toward the stage where Hanley stood gaping.

"Jump in!" he yelled. "She's only got about ten
minutes start. Maybe we can still catch her."

Hanley took his words literally and jumped. His heavier weight rocked the craft badly but it only shipped a little water. Valentine opened up the motor and the craft shot ahead through the winding waterway.

If they had come through the devious turns of the hidden stream rapidly the first time this trip was like lightning. Hanley crouched in the back, watching the spray fly past him, dodging the tree branches under which they raced.

"You think we can stop her?" he yelled to Valentine.

"We'll have to try. Maybe the other barge can do it. But if she tells the Hags where the Donovan city is hidden it means war. And we'll lose!"

Abruptly they were at the end of the concealed waterway. The canalcraft burst through the low fronds of the tangletree, then made a wide arc as Valentine turned it toward distant Nard. Both men strained their eyes. The barge of the Donovan guards was skirting the bank on the other side of the stream. There was not a trace of the girl's craft in all the length of the waterway.

"She got away!" Hanley gritted.

Valentine shook his head puzzledly. "She must have. But I don't see how. The canal is straight here for miles. She didn't have that much lead. Unless . . ."

He swung the craft around, slanted in toward the other barge. The men in it were peering under every low-hanging bush and tree at the shoreline.

"Any sign of her?" Valentine called.

"Not a trace," the man at the controls of the other barge yelled back. "But she's got to be here. She didn't have time to get all the way down the canal. We'll find her!"

They didn't. They scoured every suspicious-looking clump of bushes for a mile in either direction but they didn't find her. After half an hour, Valentine beckoned to the other barge and they met in midstream.

"Keep on looking," Valentine ordered. "It looks as though, somehow or other, she got away—but keep looking."

"What are you going to do, Valentine?"

He said grimly, "If she does get to Nard sooner or later she'll go to the Hags. So we'll go to Nard now—and stop her!"

6

Hag-Bound

Not without apprehension the two lashed their craft to the canalside at the outskirts of the city and walked in.

It seemed their apprehension was groundless. They walked to the canalmen's bar where they had been the night before—ever so long before—without untoward event.

It was early afternoon. The place was empty of customers. On one side tables were stacked and the floor was being cleaned. Darl and her dancing partner were going through a new routine to the music of a disgruntled pianist. When Darl caught sight of the newcomers her eyes widened sharply and she broke step, colliding with her partner.

She walked over to Valentine. "I'm honored," she said. "This is the first time you've come here in the day."

"We came to find out something," Valentine said seriously. "Darl, did you say last night that you'd seen that Earthgirl before?"

"Why, yes. She's been here several time."

"Do you know where she lives?"

"No. Or—wait. Yes, I do. She's staying at the Marabek. At least I think that's the hotel. I heard her mention it to the ensign last night."

"Good girl!" Valentine applauded. "Well, thanks. I'll be seeing you."

"Wait a moment!" Darl said stormily. "I'm going with you. I want to know what this is all about."

"Now, Darl . . ."

"I want to know! Last night you maneuvered around until you got a chance to talk to her, then you left the same time she did. Now you're going to visit her. Well, I'm going along."

"Wait a minute, Darl," Hanley interrupted. "Honest, this isn't a romance. Valentine has to keep her from telling something to . . ." he halted. Darl wasn't looking at him. Wide-eyed and frightened, she stared at Valentine.

"I guess I talk too much," Hanley finished embarrassedly.

Valentine snorted. "I guess you do," he agreed. "Darl, I'll tell you the whole story later. Right now I can't."

"Oh, no," Darl said quickly. "Valentine, I knew you were in trouble. The Hags were after you last night. You've got to let me help you. I can help—there must be something. Maybe she won't let you see her. Maybe I can go to her and do whatever you want me to do."

"There's something in what you say," Valentine admitted. He sighed. Earnestly he said, "Darl, you may be getting into serious trouble. Do you realize that?"

She nodded.

Valentine spread his hands. "Then come along," he said. "I didn't want to mix you up in this but I guess I've got to."

Darl's ground-car was parked just around the corner. She made hasty excuses to her partner and the pianist and they started for the Marabek. When the car was moving Darl spoke.

"Can't you tell me something about this, please, Valentine? I'm worried about you."

Valentine grimaced ruefully. He said, "I've spilled more secrets in the past twenty-four hours than all the rest of the Donovans have in a hundred and fifty years. I guess I can tell one more."

"The Donovans!" Darl echoed. "I thought there was . . . oh, Valentine!"

"Yes, I'm a Donovan," Valentine admitted. "And the Hags would make it worthwhile for anyone who told them so!"

"I'd never tell! I couldn't. And you know how I feel about the Hags. Ever since they came and took me to that awful Palace, and kept me there so long and asked me all those questions."

Valentine nodded. "I'm not worried about you," he said. "But the Earthgirl's a different matter. She knows—and she'll be happy to talk. We had a little run-in last night."

"Oh?"

"In fact, I practically kidnaped her. I had her in a safe place and she got away. I have to get her again before she sees the Hags."

"But can't you hide or runaway—out into the swamps?"

Valentine shook his head. "That wouldn't even save my own life," he said gently. "And there's much more at stake."

Hanley said, "We followed her in this morning from that safe place Valentine mentioned. She knows where it is, see?"

Darl bit her lip. "Well," she said presently, "what shall we do? We're only a few blocks from the Marabek—and there's the Hag Palace, right ahead."

"Go to the hotel," Valentine ordered. "Maybe we can find out at the desk whether she's back." He cast a quizzical look at the looming white tower of the Hag Palace. "I can't say I like getting so close to our friends there," he murmured. "Maybe we'd better—hold it! Look!"

*   *   *

He was erect, pointing out the window of the ground car. Darl gasped and the car swerved under her hand. She brought it to a halt.

"It's the girl!"

Hanley stared. "What's she doing here? You think she's going to the Palace?"

Valentine wasted no time. "We can't take any chances. Stay here, both of you, and watch what happens. I'm going to try to stop her!"

"*Wait!*" Darl wailed but Valentine was out of the car already. Even faster than his body moved his mind was racing—trying to find a plan, a method of kidnapping the girl on the crowded street. On impulse he called to her, "Elena! Elena Orris!"

She was perhaps a dozen yards from him, walking toward the Hag Palace. There was no hurry in her walk. Valentine found time to wonder at that—and then she turned in answer to his call.

Her eyes widened in recognition and her hand flew to her mouth. Instantly she turned, began to run. Valentine, cursing under his breath, ran after her. He was faster than she but they were almost at the entrance of the cloud-high, stalagmitic tower of the Hags and he hadn't the slightest chance of stopping her.

And he was amazed. The girl raced past the entrance without a glance, ran on down the block. Astonishment made him falter, then he saw something which stopped him in his tracks. From the door between the girl and himself came a rushing clatter, and then a group of robots hurtled out, half a dozen of them. Without stopping to look around they raced toward him!

He had only a split second in which to think and act. It was not enough. Frenziedly he grappled for the disklike affair in his pocket to try the desperate gamble of pitting it against the oncoming monsters but it was too late.

Instantly they were around him. He grunted in pain as the snakelike tenacles of one whipped about his body, squeezing him in a metallic embrace. His hands were pinioned hopelessly and the pocket with the disk was out of reach.

He was lifted into the air. He caught a faint glimpse in his gyrations of the couple he had left, standing paralyzed next to the ground car, watching him. Then the robot rattled and bumped along the street and bore him, helpless, through the open gateway of the Hag Palace . . .

Valentine stared into the eyes of the hawk-faced woman. She was the one who had been in the café, he noted wearily. The robot completed its rough, thorough search of him and bore the trophies to the Hag.

The woman laughed harshly and picked up the silvery disk. "Another one," she said. "We're making quite a collection." She tossed it down contemptuously and leaned forward, staring at him.

"Valentine of the Donovans," she said, "I suppose you know where you are."

"Yes."

"And do you know what is going to happen to you?"

"I have a fair idea," he admitted.

She shook her head silently. "No," she said. "No, you don't have any idea at all. I understand you Donovans aren't as skilled in—shall we say, punishment?—as we."

Valentine stirred restlessly. He said, "Of course we aren't. I confess I don't expect to leave here alive."

She said contemptuously, "Is that all? You don't understand. We probably shan't kill you."

Valentine stiffened silently. *Torture*, he thought— torture to make him tell what they wanted, torture for the sake of their holy science, torture for the love of torture itself . . .

The woman smiled satisfiedly as she saw that he understood. She made as if to rise, then hesitated.

"There are a few minor questions," she said, "I don't think you'll mind answering them. Suppose we get them cleared up before we ask the important ones."

Play for time, Valentine thought. Aloud he said, "Let's hear them."

"What were you doing in the dirty little café?"

"Visiting a friend. What were you doing?" he countered.

She raised her eyebrows imperiously but answered. "We were looking for you. Unfortunately we let you get away."

"What did you want me for?" Valentine asked.

The Hag smiled maliciously and shook her head. "No," she said. "*You* answer the questions. Who was the friend?"

Valentine hesitated, then said, "The dancer. Her name is Darl." After all, he thought, they must know that much already.

"Why?"

"Why?" he repeated. "Because I'm a man and she's a beautiful girl. Do you understand a thing like that?"

"I understand it," the Hag said grimly. "I need not believe it." Abruptly she shrugged and stood up. Imperiously, "It will be simpler to ask you questions later. Follow me."

She walked out of the room, not even looking around to see if he followed. With her unarmed back before him and no other person in sight a quick, furtive gleam of hope danced in his mind—a dream of a break for freedom. But it paled and died as he heard the clattering steps of the robot behind him. The woman, he ruefully admitted to himself, took no chances.

It was a short walk. Valentine had a brief glimpse of gray-walled corridors that seemed endless, then they were at the entrance to a large room. Over the woman's slight shoulder as they walked in, Valentine saw rows of steel-barred cages along one wall, flat, white-topped tables that looked ominously like a surgery, a pair of brooding Hags watching them.

In a husky voice like an old man's the smaller of the two waiting Hags asked, "Is this the Donovan?"

"Yes," answered the one with Valentine. "You can take him as soon as you're ready. He—"

She was interrupted by an agonized scream from within the room. Loud, shrill, horrid, the sound seemed

to startle even the Hags. The small one gasped
something and whirled, ran to one of the cages along the
wall, her long skirts flapping around her sticklike legs.
She fumbled briefly with an intricate sort of catch, then
flung the door open and rushed in.

Valentine, startled enough almost to forget his peril,
followed her curiously. Inside the cell she was bending
over a body—a human body, Valentine saw with a thrill
of horror. As he caught sight of it, it writhed
spasmodically and there was another shriek louder than
before, dwindling into a bubbling guttural. Then the
half hidden body slumped and relaxed and the ululation
ceased.

With an exclamation of disgust the Hag rose and
came out of the cell. She stamped her foot petulantly—and Valentine thought the womanly gesture
singularly horrible in that caricature of a female.

"The third one," she said bitterly. "I thought for a
while that she'd live—but she died the same way as the
others. I think we are a long way from success in this
series."

The Hag shrugged impatiently. "Take another subject," she said. "This is ordered. It must succeed."

She noticed Valentine's taut face and stared. Her impatience changed to arrogant amusement. "Donovan,
perhaps now you begin to understand," she purred.

White-lipped, in anger as much as apprehension,
Donovan asked, "What was that?"

The Hag shrugged. "An experiment. We make many
of them. Perhaps you will be an experiment too, some
day," she said. "Would you like to avoid that?"

He raised his eyebrows skeptically. "Do I have the
choice?"

"Surely. Just open your mind to us," the Hag said.
"You Donovans are trouble to us always, out there in
the swamps, always silent and threatening. Sooner or
later we will have to destroy the Donovans. If you will
help us to do it *now*—you can live."

"And if I don't I die."

The Hag nodded.

Valentine pursed his lips. He seemed lost in thought, staring beyond her at the instrument-covered operating table. He paced absently toward it. "Well," he said thoughtfully, "none of us can live forever."

The Hag scowled and stepped back a pace. "You're a fool, Valentine! she crackled.

She might have said more but Valentine in his slow, abstracted walk, had got where he wanted to be. He was between the Hag and the door, across the operating table from the three of them. In a decimal of a second his arms slipped under the table, lifted and heaved.

With a shower of instruments it caught the three of them and bowled them over. Not pausing to see what he had done—hoping that the shattered glassware and flying scalpels had killed at least one—Valentine spun and ran lightly for the door.

It was a long gamble—and the only one he had left to make. He reached the door, rounded the corner . . .

He had only a fleeting glimpse of what was waiting for him outside and then the lunging, ponderous metal figure of the serf-robot, the forgotten, impregnable serf-robot, crushed him against the side of the door.

He never saw the tentacle that lashed down upon him. He only felt a stinging whip-crack on his scalp and then he was unconscious.

7

No Sisters to Him

There was another wasp-bite sting, this time in his nose, and Valentine was awake. The small Hag who had made the experiment was looking down at him distastefully.

Valentine struggled up on an elbow and saw that he was back in the surgical room, in one of the cells along the wall this time. The Hag reached down and grasped his wrist contemptuously. After a second's consideration of his pulse she dropped the arm and walked out of the cell.

"Stay there," she flung curtly over her shoulder.

In a moment she was back with the other Hag, the one who had interviewed him when he was first captured. She stared malignantly at Valentine, who was slumped against the wall, still dazed.

"You're meek enough now," she said. "Why don't you try to escape again?"

Valentine said tiredly, "It doesn't seem to do much good."

The Hag nodded. "If there is a next time, it will do you a lot of harm. You *hurt* three of us!"

Valentine shrugged. "Your robot didn't help me

much," he observed. Then, remembering, he put his hand to his scalp. There was no pain, no scar. Only a sort of a tingling there, and at the nape of his neck, that indicated the growth of new, healing flesh. Vita-rays, he thought wonderingly.

He said, "Thanks for the first aid. You take good care of your—ah—guests."

The Hag waved a hand impatiently. "Talk," she said. "You are given one more chance. You saw what happened to one of our subjects—and we were not trying to punish her. We wouldn't be so dispassionate in treating you."

"Oh, I wouldn't expect it."

"Now you may make your choice. Life or the laboratories."

Valentine raised his head. "What kind of life? Will you let me go free?"

"Of course not. You'll be a captive. We have need for captives sometimes. We'll make only one promise. You will live as long as you would normally and you will not be in pain."

Valentine looked at her speculatively. "You know," he said, "I'm tempted to say yes, just to see what you've got planned for me. I bet it's a beauty." Then he sighed. "But your offer isn't good enough. I'm afraid it never would be good enough either. You see, I'd rather be dead than alive on those terms."

She shrugged—and without disappointment, he saw with surprise. Anxiously she glanced at the watch strapped on her wrist before she spoke.

Valentine thought there was a curious, sardonic light flickering in her webby eyes as she said, "I'll let you think it over. You needn't stay in your cage—you may have the freedom of this laboratory. But don't try to leave it. The three cages to your right contain subjects for one of our experiments. Look them over—it may help you to decide."

She turned and walked out, closing the corridor door behind her. A wait of half a minute and Valentine was at the door. He tried the latch without hope and was not disappointed when he found it locked from outside.

He ranged the walls of the room. Opposite the cages there were only blank walls and cabinets of equipment and instruments. The wall opposite the door was mostly a huge white screen—for viewing microslides, he thought. And the cages offered no escape.

It penetrated that there was no escape. He shrugged and began a search of the cabinets. A weapon, he thought, would be valuable. It was in the third cabinet that he found the workbook. He glanced at it incuriously, was about to toss it back on the shelf when a fluttering page caught his eyes. He picked it up and read:

> Your progress unsatisfactory. The ship is ready and will be dispatched for Ganymede colony within thirty days. It is imperative that we have true-breeding specimens for labor by then.

He frowned at the jagged script. Ganymede colony—were the Hags planning to spread their authority to another planet? And what sort of "true-breeding specimens" were meant?

He opened the book and examined it hurriedly. There was page after page of a sort of shorthand, an abbreviated technical jargon concerning some biological experiments being made. He puzzled over a diagram which showed a human circulatory and respiratory system but with what looked to be a sort of gill arrangement instead of the nose-and-lung of mankind.

A neatly lettered table in the back of the book was more enlightening—and hopeful. It said simply:

```
2314---840   Novitiates.
2315---798   Novitiates.
2316---781   Novitiates.
2317---778   Novitiates.
2318---742   Novitiates.
2319---708   Novitiates.
2320---675   Novitiates.
```

2321---596   Novitiates.
2322---489   Novitiates.
2323---312   Novitiates.

Valentine shook his head, hardly able to believe it. It was true—less and less had the Hags come out in public within the past years—but it was hard to believe that the reason was that they were dying out! And if it were true—at the present rate another five years would see them extinct!

He was distracted from this pleasurable thought by a sort of flopping noise coming from one of the cages. He walked over to peer into it—and stood fast, incredulous and sickened. A sodden lump of flesh lay on the floor, rhythmically arching its body, then relaxing with a flop. Over and over it repeated the slow, brainless motion, its face upturned blindly to the ceiling—if the eyeless, noseless mass of flesh below the hairline could properly be called a face. And the body to which it was attached . . .

He turned back, revolted and burning with fury. He gave the subjects in the other cages only a split-second glance—just long enough to see that they were beyond help from him. Was that, he wondered, why the Hag had left him alone? So that he could look at them, and be frightened into obedience?

He could see no reason to doubt it—none but a deep conviction that the Hags were never obvious and a puzzled memory of the glint of malicious laughter he had seen in her eyes.

Valentine paused no longer. He walked quickly to the instrument cabinets and looked over the array of surgical tools inside. He chose a lean bistoury with a flat, razor-like blade and a handle that fitted his palm and walked to the locked door. His plan was far from concrete in his mind as he stood there, patient, waiting for what might enter.

Plan? He had no plan. Everything would depend, he thought dully, on the foresight of the Hag. If she came alone—then there was a slim, slim chance for life. If she came with one other and was just a little bit careless in

her arrogance there would be a chance for revenge. But
if she came cautiously and made no mistakes—then
there was only a chance for death.

He remembered the uncanny medical skill of the Hags
and realized that even death was not sure. A second's
hesitation—a gash that cut not quite deep enough—and
they could bring him back to life on their surgical tables.
And that was a chance he could not afford to take.

His wait was not very long. He had just begun to tire
of his position of rigid attention when there was a
premonitory click and the door abruptly swung open.
Valentine tensed for the spring, peering at the opening.
Luck—there was only a single Hag. But as he was about
to leap another figure appeared from behind her,
holding a drawn ray-pencil. Stunned, Valentine recognized Darl! She was smiling, almost weeping in relief.

"Hurry, Valentine," she whispered. "Thank heaven
I got here in time!"

Valentine wasted no time. He drew the pair inside the
door, closed it. With the straps on the surgery tables he
bound the Hag, and gagged her with a strip torn from
her own white robes. He carried her to one of the cages,
dropped her none too gently inside. Then he turned to
face Darl.

"You're wonderful," he said simply. "Tell me how
you got here—but not now. Now we have to get out. Do
you know the way?"

Darl nodded. "The way we came—if there aren't any
Hags around. I thought we could take this one with us,
and if anybody saw us they'd think we working for her
or something."

Valentine shook his head. "Too many of them know
what I look like. We'll have to try to stay out of sight,
that's all. Lead the way."

Darl peered out into the hall, then motioned to him to
follow. They hurried down the corridor, past the room
where Valentine had been carried by the robot, to the
elevators. Darl pressed the button and they waited for a
silent second.

A clattering sound came down the corridor.

"A robot," Darl whispered, "Valentine!"

He stared about, saw a door ajar and tugged her toward it. They were inside just as he caught a glimpse of the thing rounding a corner toward them.

"Did it see us?" she whispered.

"I hope not." Valentine turned to inspect his surroundings. They were in a little anteroom. He saw another door and moved silently toward it, peered around the frame into the room beyond.

It was a long, narrow room with both long walls lined with telescreen after telescreen, all going at once. Before each screen was a photorecorder, and a Hag was moving along the line of screens, examining them. She was absorbed in what she was doing, Valentine thought, and the buzz of the sounds from the screen would cover any slight noise they might make.

He leaned out a little further, craning his neck to see what was on the screens. Oddly, they didn't seem used for communication. The nearest one showed only dim, flickering lights with no shape or substance. The second was a book, magnified in the foreground of the screen. It, too, flickered—part of the page becoming brighter and the rest dimmer from time to time.

The whole scene jerked around in the screen occasionally, as though the telecaster had been jarred by an incautious elbow. Valentine tried to make out the background of the scene but without success. It was curiously dim and blurred, worse than the usual out-of-focusness.

The Hag halted abruptly, staring at one of the screens in consternation. He tried to see what had made her excited. He caught only a glimpse of a woman's figure and a mechanical gadget in the screen. Then she had thrown a switch and the screen was blank. The scene, he thought puzzledly, had a peculiar quality to it. It was something he had seen . . .

Over the drone of tiny voices from the screens he heard the clatter in the hall, recalling him to his predicament. He moved to Darl's side, stood tensely while the pounding metallic feet came closer . . . and moved on past without interruption. They grew fainter, and finally faded out entirely.

"Good!" he framed with his lips for Darl. He opened the door cautiously and stepped outside. The elevator door was open and no one was in sight.

They dropped rapidly in the shaft. Valentine belatedly took the ray-pencil from Darl's hand. He held it half-concealed against his side as the elevator stopped and the door opened. There was still no one in sight. Incredible luck—thought Valentine and turned toward the daylight that shone through a door at the end of the corridor. They emerged into the court that was the main entrance to the Palace. And there luck deserted them.

There was a cargo-car parked in the court, and walking slowly around it was the massive shape of a robot. Valentine instinctively braced himself for the hopeless struggle—but there was none! Apparently the robot was only a guard for the goods-car. Surely its myriad eyes had seen them. But it merely continued its even mechanical march around the car.

Valentine asked no questions. Trying to seem as unconcerned as possible he led Darl out the entrance, down the street to where Hanley sat in the parked ground car, waiting for them.

8

"Bring in the Donovans"

They were blocks away before Valentine could sit back and relax.

"Give me a cigarette, Hanley," he said. "They picked my pockets in there."

He lit it and inhaled the pungent smoke with satisfaction. He stared at Darl through the fumes.

"I owe you my life," he said. "Thanks. Tell me how you did it."

"It wasn't very hard," Darl confessed. "I—I knew the place a little bit from the last time I was there. I just went back to the café and got the cashier's ray-pencil, and came in and got you. I ran into that Hag the first thing, so I brought her along."

Valentine shook his head wonderingly. "Marvelous girl," he said. "Well, let's get moving. There is work to be done."

"What do we do?" Hanley called over his shoulder, from the wheel.

"We go through with the original plan. Take us to the Marabek—you still going through with this, Darl?"

She nodded silently.

"Good. We'll get out there and you do a little scouting job. I want you to go down to that Earth storehouse and see if you can find out whether the Hags have taken it over. If possible get a couple of the disks—the Hags took mine away from me. But don't get in any trouble and meet us in the dining room of the Marabek in—well, let's say an hour."

Hanley nodded. "Okay," he said resignedly. "Don't think I'm going to enjoy it, though. It seems to me they'll find out you're gone some time soon."

"I thought of that," Valentine agreed. "That's a chance we have to take."

Hanley paused in front of the mammoth hotel just long enough for Valentine and the girl to get out, then was off toward the canalfront.

The covering clouds overhead were turning gray with sunset as they entered the hotel. With Darl on his arm Valentine strolled in a leisurely fashion toward the dining room, unobtrusively noticing every person in the lobby.

As they passed the desk he paused and said to Darl, "Excuse me for a second." Then, to the clerk, "Is Miss Elena Orris in her room?"

The man picked up a cradle phone and spoke into it. There was a brief wait, and then he spoke, shaking his head. "I'm sorry, sir. May I take a message?"

"Oh, I think not," Valentine said casually. "We'll be here for a while—I'll try later. By the way, what's her room number?"

"Twenty thirty-seven," said the clerk. Valentine thanked him politely and escorted Darl to the dining room. As the headwaiter came up he selected a table and pointed to it. The functionary gave him a sizing-up glance, then bowed and led them to the chosen spot.

It was near neither the orchestra nor the thinly-populated dance floor but it had a tremendous vir-tue—it was partly screened by a potted fern-tree, and there were no tables behind it, only a small alternate entrance to the dining room.

Darl and Valentine sat facing the dark floor. The waiter brought them thin glasses of greenish flower-dew, waited while Valentine ordered a meal. The restaurant surroundings reminded him that he hadn't eaten for hours—days, if one counted the time spent under the Hags' vita-rays at its true value.

When the waiter had gone Darl said, "No one can hear what we say now, can they."

Valentine lifted his glass, smiling gently. "I suppose not. What do you want to talk about?"

She returned the smile but her voice had no laughter in it. She said, "Oh, Valentine, I'm worried!" The dancer's professional smile stayed on her face for the benefit of whoever might look but her voice was dangerously close to breaking.

Valentine said softly, "I won't lie to you. I'm worried too."

She stared at him for a bleak moment. Then the smile, which had wavered, came back. She lifted her glass to touch his. They drank ceremoniously . . . and then the waiter came back with the food.

When they had eaten and were sipping their thick, black swamplands coffee Valentine spoke seriously again.

"The vacation's over," he said abruptly. "Now we get back to work. I've got to see Elena Orris."

Darl nodded. "What are we going to do?"

He gestured to the waiter, asked for a phone. "Call her for me," he asked Darl. "She won't recognize your voice. Tell her you have to see her."

The waiter brought the phone and plugged it in. Darl picked it up hesitantly, looking at Valentine for help.

"Room twenty thirty-seven," he supplied "Please . . ."

Darl frowned but took the phone and spoke into it. She listened for a second, then sang, "Hello . . . Oh, she isn't? Thank you," and put it back in its cradle.

"She still isn't in," she told Valentine. "I'm not

sorry. I don't know what I would have said to her."

Valentine ran a hand through his hair. He said, "But suppose I made a mistake. Suppose she doesn't come back to her room tonight."

Darl's annoyance faded. Her tawny eyes were large as she said, "Oh, Valentine, I'm sorry. Can't we wait here or something until she comes?"

"We might as well," Valentine said dourly. The waiter returned to remove the phone. Valentine watched him silently until he began to walk away, then snapped to life and called the man back.

"Two more flower-dews," he ordered. To Darl, "We might as well make a party of it. We'll drink this round to Elena Orris."

"Then you'd better order another," said a deep female voice from behind him. "I'll drink one to myself!"

Valentine stifled a grunt of surprise as Elena Orris walked around from behind him. She gestured to the waiter to bring another chair. There was cocksure confidence in her manner as she faced Valentine.

"They told me at the desk someone had called my room from here. I had a ghost of an idea it might be you so I came in the side door." She turned her eyes to Darl, studying her curiously. "Oh, I know you," she said. "You're the dancer, aren't you?"

Darl said evenly, "I dance at the Golden Nard. Do you earn your own living?"

"A point," conceded Elena Orris. "Well, let's talk about something else. Valentine, why have you been looking for me?"

Valentine shrugged. He said, "That's pretty obvious. You know where the Donovan city is, and I don't want you to tell the Hags."

Elena Orris smiled as the waiter came up with the fresh drinks. When he had gone she said over the rim of her glass, "You're a little late. I've had eighteen hours in which to tell them if I wanted to."

He said dryly, "I was unavoidably detained. Do you mean you haven't tried to tell them?"

"I haven't. I wish you'd trust me, Valentine. I told you—Earth wants the Donovans for an ally."

Valentine said slowly, "Maybe you're lying again. But if you are it's too late for me to do anything about it."

"Correct," said the girl. "So you might as well assume I'm playing fair. Is there any reason why we can't be allies?"

Valentine said honestly, "I don't know if we can trust you. Earth has a bad record."

The girl said impatiently, "I told you what we want—mining concessions and trade. What do you have to lose?"

"Very little," Valentine admitted.

"That's right. It was different out in the swamps. You could keep me there, and your secret was safe. But I escaped."

"That raises an interesting point," Valentine said. "*How* did you get away?"

The girl smiled. "I took the anesthetic away from your surgeon."

"I know that. I mean, after you got in the barge."

"Oh. Well, I just started it and kept going until I came out in a canal. Then I stopped a canalcraft and asked them the way to Nard. He gave me directions. I went straight ahead for six miles, then left where the canals forked and left again—"

Valentine started at her. "You *what?* Which way did you turn, coming out of the Donovan city?"

"Why right, of course."

Valentine leaned back, still staring. He shook his head ruefully after a moment. He said almost to himself, "I guess it was an easy mistake to make—but we were idiots, all the same. We forgot there were two directions on the waterway. We headed for Nard and you were going there by the long way around! No wonder we couldn't catch you!"

"Was that the wrong way? I'd never seen it before, you see."

Valentine said resignedly. "Never mind. Go ahead

with your story. You were persuading me we ought to be allies."

The girl shrugged irritably. "That's all. If I haven't talked you into it by now I give up. Help us and we'll help you. Refuse—and you know very well the Hags will wipe you out."

Valentine said, conversationally, "Of course, I could kill you and keep you from telling the Hags that way. I might even be able to get out of Nard alive, that way."

The girl shook her head. "It wouldn't do you any good. I'm not the only one who knows."

Valentine scanned her narrowly. "I suppose that means you told the ensign about it. Well, it would be a little harder but I could kill him too."

She wavered, but clung gamely to the argument. "I doubt if you could find him—I told him to stay hidden. Even if you did, you wouldn't be sure. And you can't afford to take that big a chance."

Valentine admitted defeat. "All right," he said abruptly. "Let's talk business. We're allies—I can speak for the Council of the Donovans."

The girl exhaled deeply and raised her glass again. "A toast to our alliance!" she proposed and drank. Then, "I'll tell you the whole story," she said. "She took one of the wavetraps out of her handbag and tossed it on the table.

"You know what these things are. You operate them—so." She touched a tiny stud projecting from the rim of the disk. Valentine thought he heard a faint, faint hum before she pushed the stud back into place and the sound died. "They take any radio wave within range, suck it in and rebroadcast it as static. It's not just a radio receiver—it *attracts* radio waves. It will even break in on a sealed beam such as the Hags use for their robots. And the effective radius of action is about fifty feet."

"Suppose they change frequencies?" Valentine asked.

"It doesn't matter. This isn't selective—any wave length will work it."

"And what happens to the robot?"

"It depends on what it's doing when it comes within range. If it's just standing still, nothing happens. It keeps on standing there and you can walk up to it and defuse it. If it's moving it will probably keep on moving until it runs into something or falls down. But it can't be controlled any more by the Hags."

Valentine nodded, reached out and touched the thing. The hum began. He listened to it curiously, then said, "When does the attack come off? Are the rest of the Earthmen ready?"

"They're ready. The attack is planned for tomorrow!"

"Tomorrow! And what do you want us to do?"

"Bring in the Donovans! Let them help us do the fighting. We'll give them wavetraps, fight side by side with them against the Hags."

Valentine, face suddenly tense, said, "I forgot to ask you. Do you know that the Hags found out about the wavetraps? Apparently they found them in the warehouse last night."

"I know," Elena said. "Ensign Drake told me all about it. The robots were buzzing around there like flies. They took a crate of the traps to the Hag Palace and left a robot guarding the door so we can't get at what's left. He was watching from across the street."

"Fine," Valentine said disgustedly. "What does that do to our plans?"

"Why, nothing at all. We only had about a thousand traps in the warehouse. We have six times as many hidden away."

"Where?"

She hesitated. "They're—in a safe place," she said finally. "Maybe it's better if I don't tell you where. That's how secrets leak out."

Valentine nodded slowly. "All right. Just so you get them to us when we need them." He sat up straighter, reached out for the disk and held it for a second before clicking it off.

"It sounds all right," he said. "You agree not to make any demands for Earth beyond the mining rights?"

"That's all. We have to have them, Valentine. Venus is the last rich source of carnotite, and Earth needs uranium."

Valentine said abruptly, "We'll do it." He paused, thinking rapidly. "I can get back to the Donovan city in two hours. Say it takes me four hours to get a thousand men together, then another two hours to bring them back. We'll pick up the gadgets on the way and be here and ready by daybreak."

The girl stood up, her face flushed, the sparkle of high adventure in her eyes. She said, "I'll find Ensign Drake and tell him to get everything ready. We'll meet you at the waterfront at the south end of the city—an hour before sunrise!"

She picked up the disk, turned and hurried out without another word. Valentine followed her with troubled eyes.

Darl asked, "Can we trust her, Valentine? These Earthpeople . . ."

"I wish I knew," he said wearily. "Heaven knows she's right in what she says. We have nothing to lose—but I just can't trust Earth."

He glanced at his wrist watch. "Hanley's overdue," he said. "We'll give him ten more minutes, then I'll have to start out for the city. It's going to be difficult enough without wasting any more time . . ."

But it was less than ten minutes when Hanley appeared—only a matter of seconds after the Earthgirl had left.

There was anxiety in his chunky face as he stared around the dining room for them. When he spied them he hurried over.

Valentine rose instinctively to meet him. "What's the matter?" he asked crisply.

Hanley groaned, "Elena Orris—that's the matter. I saw her coming out just as I was coming in. She was a prisoner, with a robot holding onto her. They took her toward the Hag Palace!"

9

Time to Move

Valentine stood fast, but it seemed the room spun around him. Success had opened up to him where he had expected only failure—and then it had been snatched away.

He sank down into his chair. All he said was, "Lord!"

Quickly, sympathetically, Darl touched his hand. "I know, Valentine," she whispered. "It looked good for a second."

"I can't understand it," he said dazedly. "If they knew she was connected with this revolt—or knew that she had information on the Donovan city—why didn't they pick her up before? Why didn't they get her this morning, when they jumped me? It's almost as though they knew everything that was going on and were giving us enough rope to hang ourselves."

Darl shook her head despondently.

Hanley said, "Listen, maybe they have this place wired up, Valentine! Maybe they've been listening in on what's been said here!"

Valentine snapped to attention, his eyes darting

about. Then he slumped back. "No," he said. "They couldn't wire every table in the city—and they didn't know we'd sit at this one." He held up his hand. "Please," he begged. "Let me think this over for a second. Part of this just doesn't make sense."

The two watched him with bated breath. He sat motionless, staring into space, revolving ideas in his mind. Somehow the pieces could be fitted together, he thought. Somewhere there was a solution that could save them. The wavetraps, and the robots and the Earth plan for revolt . . .

The Hags knew more than he had imagined, he realized. That morning the robots had come boiling out of the Palace as though they knew what they were after. There had been no looking around for him, no indecision. And his escape was peculiar.

It was peculiar that Darl had made a single-handed entry into the supposedly impregnable palace, and succeeded.

"Let's get out of here," he said suddenly. "I want to see something." They paid their check and left. It was dark night outside with only the fluorescents of the city casting a glow upon the clouds overhead. They got in Darl's parked ground car, Hanley at the wheel.

"Drive down to the canal where we left the barge," Valentine ordered. "If it's still there maybe we can get through to the Donovans. But I'm not very hopeful."

And his despair was justified. Hanley wheeled the vehicle down to the waterfront and there before them was the spot where they had left the canalcraft. It was still there—but standing impassive guard before it was a serf-robot, silent and waiting. And out in the stream they could see the lights of patrolling canalcraft, could make out the jagged outlines of the mechanical monsters who were their crews.

Hanley drove past the moored canalcraft at an even pace, to avoid attracting attention, then turned another corner and slowed.

"It looks bad," he said over his shoulder. "It looks like they're waiting for us."

Soberly Valentine nodded. "I was afraid of it," he said. "Now I think we're beaten."

His mind was surprisingly calm. He accepted the fact of defeat. It was there and nothing could be done about it. The girl and the wavetraps could have saved them but the Hags had her captive. And the disks were guarded—he had glimpsed the robot as they drove past.

The Hags had Elena Orris. She was not the type to talk easily—but they would not be as humane as he and she would talk in the end. When the Hags had the location of the Donovan city from her the robots would come . . .

He mused idly upon the curious callousness of the robots, steel and plastic simulacra of humanity. If it had been human warriors fighting for the Hags there might have been a chance. But against the machines—never. And the tiny new ones the Hags seemed to be building now, the receptors they had found in the crashed plane—what were they like? They were so small, small enough to be lost in a garment, or a fold of flesh.

He sat bolt upright and Darl stared at him.

"What's the matter, Valentine?" she asked querulously.

He stared at her in abstraction. "Nothing," he said finally. "I just . . . nothing."

In his mind was a vision and he clung to it, fascinated.

It was a line of telescreens like those he had seen in the Hag Palace, and before the screens a Hag was watching. The brief glimpse he had caught of the scenes portrayed—the mystifying scenes that seemed to be the wheel of a ground car and the pages of a book and the blurred vision of a scene oddly like the one he himself was looking at . . .

"Give me a pencil and paper," he said.

Darl, staring at him curiously, fumbled in her bag and brought out a notebook. "I'll light the dome light," she said, reaching for the switch. But Valentine stopped her.

"Never mind the light," he said.

Darl watched him with deep apprehension. His eyes were fixed on the back of Hanley's head before them and the notebook was in his lap. His hand was painfully printing on the page of the book in the slow, agonized manner of a blind man. She peered to see what he was writing but his big hand covered the page.

After a few moments he ripped the page out, still without looking at it, and folded it once. He handed back the notebook and pencil.

"What was I saying?" he asked.

She sat upright in the seat, half facing him. "Tell me what you're thinking!" she demanded.

Valentine took her hand gently. "I'm sorry, Darl," he said. "I was upset for a while. Now it's all right."

"All *right!*" she gasped. "With the Hags ready to wipe out the Donovans, searching the city for you—"

"Darl, if you had heard just twenty-four hours ago that the Hags had wiped out the Donovans, what would it have meant to you?"

"Why—nothing, I guess," she confessed. "But that was yesterday!"

"And today it's the same," Valentine said persuasively. "What would you say if I told you that we can live in peace, you and I together?"

Her eyes opened wider than ever and her jaw unbeautifully dropped. She faced him without words, searching his face in the darkness. She could see lines of strain lurking behind the impassiveness.

"We can do it, Darl," he said. "The Hags made me an offer today. My life in exchange for information. Since they'll have the information soon anyhow I might as well give in. You see, we're beaten, Darl. We haven't got much left and we can't afford to lose what we've got."

There was a shriek of brakes and an abrupt swerve. Hanley brought the ground car to a stop, turned and faced them.

"What the heck, Valentine!" he exploded. "I heard that!"

Valentine released Darl and leaned forward, his face drawn with obscure emotions. He placed a hand on

Hanley's shoulder and said tersely, "What else can we do? Think it over—don't say anything yet."

Hanley's furious expression turned to perplexity and he gazed down into his lap. Valentine hastily sat back.

"While you're thinking, Hanley," he said, "you might as well drive us around. I don't know how much more freedom we're going to have and I want to make the most of mine."

Valentine placed an arm around Darl's shoulders, drew her to him. She struggled free, almost weeping. "I don't understand," she said.

Valentine sighed and narrowed his eyes. "Darl, Hanley said something to me the other night. He said you were in love with me. Tell me whether he was right or wrong."

Color leaped into her marble cheeks. She said, "He was right, Valentine."

He swallowed convulsively. "Then trust me," he ordered. "Lean back—here." He drew her to him. "Close your eyes, Darl. I want to tell you something." Gently his fingers crept around her small head, touched the lids of her eyes to make sure they were closed.

Valentine shut his own eyes and spoke to her softly. "I could never tell you that I loved you before, Darl," he whispered. "Not while I was a Donovan and an outlaw. I couldn't ask a woman to share the risk. But now . . ."

He spoke on and on, and gradually the tenseness in the girl's slim figure subsided and she clung to him. "Don't open your eyes," he whispered, and took his hand away. It was only then that he found his hand was damp . . . with her silent tears.

In the front seat Hanley frowned and read over again the note that Valentine had surreptitiously dropped in his lap. He shrugged hopelessly, then with determination crumpled it, flung it out the window and started the car again. After a moment the frown disappeared and his face began almost to wear a smile.

At least, he was thinking, there would be a fight!

*   *   *

The car slowed down and Hanley's voice came back to them.

"Valentine," he said tentatively, "Valentine, we're there now. Are you sure about this?"

Valentine said exultantly, "Is the robot still guarding the entrance?"

"Yep."

"Just one—no others close enough to do us any damage right away?"

"Well—the one across the street. But we'll have half a minute, or so, before it can get here."

"Fine!" Valentine released the girl. He yelled, "Go ahead, Hanley! Plow into him!"

The car surged forward as Hanley trod on the accelerator, swerved around in a tight arc and smashed into something with a vast cacophony.

Darl's eyes flew open as she was catapulted forward in her seat. Valentine caught her as the car ground to a stop and she stared around. "Why, we're back at the warehouse!" she gasped. "What's happening?"

But Valentine was no longer beside her to hear. He was up and out of the car, followed closely by Hanley. She heard his exultant yell, "*Got* him! Good man, Hanley—come on!" and saw the two of them run into the warehouse.

Then she saw what he was gloating over—what Hanley had done. A serf-robot, feebly waving its tentacles, was pinned between the collision-bumper of the car and the corner of the building. It was not destroyed but it could not do them any damage and Darl began to understand what Hanley had done. They couldn't challenge the serf-robot on foot but the momentum of the heavy, hurtling ground-car had done what their feeble human strength could not.

Still—there were the other robots. Darl, stricken by the thought, whirled to look at the robot which had been guarding the canalcraft at the wharf down the street. And just in time—it was racing toward her, tentacles flailing the air.

Darl didn't stop to think. She ran into the building,

following Valentine and Hanley. Inside was darkness except for a yellow point of light off to one side, where Hanley was holding a match flame while Valentine scrabbled around in a broken crate that had been dashed against the floor.

She ran toward him, screaming, "Run! There's a robot right behind me—oh, run, Valentine!"

But Valentine was already running—toward her. He was fumbling with one of the silvery disks as he ran. He dodged past her without a word, his expression invisible in the dark. Astonished, Darl turned to stare after him.

There was a thundering on the floor and the huge bulk of the robot hurtled through the door, whirled and sped toward them, the bright search-beam flaring from its domed body. Silhouetted between the robot and herself Darl saw Valentine halt and stand tensely waiting, caught a glitter of light from the silvery disk in his hand. The robot pounded toward him.

Then, when only a dozen yards away, it happened.

As though stricken by an invisible sledge, the robot stumbled and fell, slid along the rough wood of the warehouse floor for twice the length of a man . . . and lay motionless, its brilliant search-beam pointed straight at the ceiling.

Valentine's exultant laugh rang out. "It works!" he yelled. "The wavetraps—they really work! Hanley, Darl—fill your pockets with them. And then come on. We've got to get out of here!"

10

Into the Hag's Palace

Miraculously, the car still worked, though it bucked and bumped from an axle that had been jarred askew. But it carried them rapidly along if not in comfort.

"We're going to the Hag Palace," Valentine ordered. "And hurry. We've got a lot to do before we're out of danger."

Hanley nodded and concentrated on his driving. But Darl said dazedly, "I don't understand. Ten minutes ago you said we were hopelessly beaten. What happened?"

Gently Valentine rested a hand on her shoulder. "That was misdirection," he said. "The Hags were listening. I had to throw them off the track to give us a little time."

"Listening? How?"

"That's what puzzled me," Valentine admitted. "I couldn't understand it, at first. Then, when I thought I had it, it was fantastic, hard to believe. But it checked."

Hanley took a corner on two wheels. Over his shoulder he complained, "I don't know what you're talking about. *What* was hard to believe."

"Do you remember what I told you about the Hag ship that crashed? We found something on it—tiny little robot transmitters. At least, we thought they were for robots. But they weren't. Do you remember the telescreens we saw in the Hag Palace? Each one of those was showing a scene being picked up by one of the tiny transmitters. They were spy transmitters!"

Darl gasped. "Do you mean the Hags were listening in on everything we said with one of those things hidden in the car?"

Valentine shook his head. "Not exactly. They were just transmitters, nothing else. They didn't have photocells or microphones. All they could do was rebroadcast radio waves."

"Well then! What in the world—"

Valentine reached out and touched her hand. "That's what was so hard to believe," he said. "But the brain is a kind of a radio transmitter itself. Yours, mine, everybody's. The nerves conduct a measurable amount of electrical energy. It can be detected by a sensitive radio set. Do you begin to see now?"

She shook her head silently.

Valentine shrugged. "They rebroadcast brain waves! Everything you or I saw and heard the transmitters picked up and relayed to the Hags. Darl—remember that you told me what the Hags did to you when they took you to the Palace, and then let you go without explanation?

"You said they had given you a vita-ray treatment, after anesthetizing you. That means only one thing—an operation. I had the same experience. Do you know what the operation was? What they did to you while you were unconscious?"

Woefully—"No."

"They buried one of those transmitters in your flesh! I think it must be in the back of the neck, near the spine. That's where mine seems to be, and it's a logical place—near the brain, you see. The thing was so small you'll never notice it. Even an X-ray might not show it.

And under the vita-rays even the scar was healed before they released you. But from that moment on the Hags could see everything you were looking at with your own eyes, hear every sound that came to your ears!''

"Good heavens!" Hanley cried. "No wonder the Hags knew everything."

Darl whispered, "How awful!" Then her hand flew to the nape of her neck. "Can they still see everything?" she asked.

"No! The wavetraps protect us. They interfere with the radio communication of the spy transmitters, just as with the robots. As long as we carry the traps we're all right—and if we live through the next hour we can have one of the Donovan surgeons remove them later."

"Sounds logical," Hanley admitted from the driver's seat. "Tell me one more thing before we get to the Hag Palace—how did you know all this?"

"It was the only answer. The Hags knew things that they couldn't have known any other way. They knew where Elena Orris was and where I was. And then they let me escape—deliberately, as if they knew you were coming. They left me alone at just the proper time.

"Coincidence doesn't stretch that far, and the Hags don't make such obvious mistakes. There had to be an explanation. And there was. They *wanted* me to escape. My guess is that they expected me to make a run for the Donovan city. That would have been fatal—a thousand robots would have followed me and destroyed us all!"

"I get it," said Hanley. "Okay, Valentine—we're almost there. Now what?"

"Stop the car across the street from the Palace," Valentine ordered.

He leaped out as soon as the car had stopped, glanced around quickly. It was still dark though the dawn was not far away. Across the street loomed the Hag Palace. A robot was visible at the entrance a hundred yards away. Satisfied that there was no immediate danger, Valentine turned back to the car.

"We're in a bad spot," he told the others. "I don't know just how we're going to do it but we have to get Elena Orris out of there."

"How?" asked Hanley.

"I don't know," Valentine confessed.

Uneasily Hanley said, "Look, Valentine, why can't we just leave her there? I know these wavetraps are great stuff but suppose something goes wrong? What would happen to the rest of the Donovans?"

Valentine shook his head. "You're right—but she's in trouble. We've got to get her out."

Hanley succumbed. "All right—but she wouldn't do it for you." He glared bitterly at the disk in his hand.

"I don't see why they couldn't have made these things a little bigger," he complained. "The way it is now, they're only good as a last resort. If they—*hey!* What's the matter?" He jumped back involuntarily as Valentine spun on him, staring.

"Say that again!" Valentine demanded.

"All I said was, these things should've been bigger. Don't scare me like that!"

Valentine shook his head wonderingly. "Hanley, you're a genius. Why didn't you think of that a little sooner?"

"Think of what?"

"Think of juicing the wavetraps up! It's very simple —with the power that they get from the built-in power-packs, they're effective at fifty feet. Twice as much power and they'll be effective twice as far. A hundred times as much power and they'll blanket the city! All we have to do is give them more power and we're in!"

"But where do we get the power?" Darl asked.

Valentine's lean face split in a grin. "From the power-packs that run this car! Get out, Hanley. Let me get at the packs."

Hanley got out, and the two of them ripped furiously at the floorboards. In a second they had exposed the dull black brick that powered the ground car. Valentine was reaching for the leads when he heard Darl's gasp.

"Valentine!" she whispered urgently. "Better hurry

up—there's a robot patrol coming this way!''

Valentine swore and straightened, staring down the street. A few hundred yards away came trotting three serf-robots. As he looked the leading robot, sweeping its search-beam from side to side, caught them in its glare.

''They saw us!'' Valentine said. They had—there was but a second's pause and then the robots swerved in their course and came hurtling toward the parked ground-car and the three fugitives.

''What'll we do?'' Hanley asked nervously. Valentine held up his hand. The three stood frozen, tensely waiting, while the robots hurtled toward them. Then they crossed the invisible line of the wavetraps' influence. They staggered—and the first one fell, the others tumbling over it and lying there like wrecked fragments of machinery.

Hanley exhaled a long sigh of relief. ''Maybe I'll get used to this in time,'' he said prayerfully, ''but that time's a long way off.''

''We aren't safe yet,'' Valentine interrupted. ''There'll be more, now that the Hags have seen us. And they may get smart enough to stay out of range and use a ray-pencil on us! Here—loosen the leads to the power-pack, while I open this disk.''

He took another wavetrap out of his pocket, turned it in his hand. There was a tiny slit next to the lever that turned it on and off. As he had seen the radio-tech do back in the Donovan city, he inserted his thumbnail in the slit and twisted. The top of the disk came off in his hand, and he was staring down into an intricate mass of wires and condensers.

Hanley had one of the power leads loose in his hand. The other was still attached to the power-pack, lying on the seat of the car. ''Suppose it's too much power and the thing burns out?'' he asked.

''It shouldn't. There aren't any tubes or filaments in it—nothing that might burn. And if it does that's the chance we take.'' Valentine frowned and lifted out a tiny cylinder, half the size of a cigarette.

''Thank heaven I watched our radio-tech take these

things apart," he said. He ripped loose the wires to the dwarf powerpack attached them gently to the leads, wrapping them securely around the contact points. He set the whole affair down on the seat of the car.

"All right, Hanley," he said. "Plug the other end of the lead in and keep your fingers crossed!"

Then he heard the familiar drumming on the pavement again. He looked up in consternation and, from the gateway of the Hag Palace down the street, saw what seemed an unending line of robots racing straight for them!

"Plug it in, Hanley!" he ordered. Hanley tore his eyes off the robots and thrust the loose end of the lead in his hand against the terminal of the power-pack. There was no faint drone this time. Instead there was a shrill buzzing as of a million tiny hornets. It was hard to realize that so much noise could come from so tiny a thing as the wavetrap—but it was working!

"Look!" gasped Darl. Like Juggernauts gone mad, the robots were hurling themselves to destruction. There must have been forty of them in the street all racing down on them in one second, and in the second that followed—destroyed.

Without the distant control of a Hag to keep them on course, most of the serf-robots merely toppled over and slid, piling up as had the three others.

Some, even after they had fallen, continued to thrash the air with their waving tentacles and limbs—still moving but no longer under control and no longer dangerous. One went careening off in a broad arc, smashing finally against the wall of a building less than a hundred feet from them.

"So far, so good," Valentine said grimly. "Now we try the hard part—fighting the Hags in their own Palace!"

11

The Trick That Took

Clutching Darl's ray-pencil, Valentine ran toward the Palace with the other two following. They skirted the prostrate forms of the robots and were inside the Palace itself before they met trouble. There was a flat hiss of sound and Valentine involuntarily flung himself to the ground.

He caught a flicker of motion in one of the corridor-entrances and fired at it. A Hag with a ray-pencil yelped and disappeared, her running footsteps echoing out to them. When he got to the entrance she was out of sight.

The three trotted down the corridor to the elevators, where Darl and Valentine had come out less than a dozen hours before. A car was waiting. But when Valentine thumbed the controls nothing happened. The controls were dead.

"They've cut the power," he said. "Well—there's no help for it. We'll have to find the stairs and climb!"

What had been an effortless trip of a few seconds in the high speed elevators of the Hags turned out to be a man-killing climb on foot even after they had found the stairs.

"You were on the fourteenth floor," Darl panted. "Maybe—Elena—will be in—the same place."

Valentine merely nodded, conserving breath. They had one more floor to go—then they heard the sound of alarm bells, a clanging that rolled toward them from all directions as every bell in the Hag Palace went off at once. A shrill female voice shrieked words that distance muffled and made impossible to understand over the annunciators.

"They're alerting the whole Palace," Valentine gasped. "Here's where the going gets tough!"

They burst out of the stairwell into the familiar gray corridor, Valentine in the lead with the ray-pencil ready. The corridor was empty. Darl pointed breathlessly down the hall.

"I think it was that fourth door," she said. Valentine nodded and raced to it—but when he flung open the door, the room was empty. He dashed to the pens that lined the wall—all were empty, even of the flopping monstrosities the Hags had created with their surgery.

Darl was about to speak but the rattle of the alarm bells drowned her out—near by this time, and so loud that they almost deafened them. There was a squeal of sound, then the shrill, peremptory female voice again.

"Warning," it shrilled. "Warning to all Novitiates. Ascend to Ship Level Immediately! The Earthies are approaching the Palace. Blast-off time in ten minutes!"

"Ship level?" Hanley repeated. "What's that?"

Valentine shrugged. "I don't know. But something's up—looks as if the Earthies have declared themselves in on the fight." He frowned. "Let's get out of here," he said. "We've got to find Elena Orris."

"Perhaps I can help you," said a harsh female voice from the corridor. "She's right down the hall."

Valentine whirled, the ray-pencil jutting out at the Hag who stood watching them. She raised her scraggly eyebrows in mock surprise.

"I have no weapon," she said. "See? All I want to do is to take you to Elena Orris."

Hanley growled, "It's a trick! Careful, Valentine!"

The Hag frowned reprovingly at him. Valentine said, "Of course it's a trick. Still—let's see what happens. We'll never find Elena by ourselves."

"That's right," said the Hag. She pointed to the door of a room across the hall. "She's right in there. The door's not locked."

Valentine, face tense, said, "You go in first. Remember, I have no compunctions about killing women. Not when they're as vicious and corrupt as you!"

The Hag snarled silently but walked ahead of them. She flung the door wide and walked steadily in. Through the door, lying supine on a couch against the wall, was Elena Orris, apparently asleep.

"Anesthetized," the Hag flung over her shoulder. "She'll come out of it in an hour or so."

Valentine started toward her, his guard momentarily down. He was well within the door before his ear caught the faint clatter of moving metal—and by the time he whirled it was too late! Hidden by the open door stood a serf-robot, unaccountably still in operation.

Before Valentine could overcome his shock the lashing tentacles had whipped about him and caught him dizzily into the air. He heard a yell from Hanley and a gasp of pain from Darl as they, too, were caught. A twisting tentacle snatched the ray-pencil from his hand . . . and they were neatly trussed and helpless.

The Hag shrieked with gloating laughter. "The very clever Donovans," she crooned. "As helpless as babes."

She strode closer, staring at Valentine. "Can you twist your head a little bit?" she asked solicitously. "Just far enough to look down at the floor. What do you see?"

Valentine looked, puzzled. There was a long, black cable snaking off to a monitor box in the wall. He wondered—then it became clear.

"I see you understand," the Hag said harshly. "Your wavetraps worked beautifully—as long as the robots were directed by radio. But you never expected us to connect one to its monitor by cable, did you?'' She laughed stridently, then stepped back and glanced at the timepiece on her wrist.

"I must hurry," she said apologetically. "The Earthies are coming—and I must be gone before they arrive." Her face darkened savagely. "You—animals," she spat. "You and the Earthies, daring to pit yourself against us! But don't think you've won! All this means is a temporary inconvenience. We'll be back. Ganymede is not so far off that we won't be able to come back. And when we return we'll stay!"

"*Ganymede!*" gasped Darl, startled into speech. "But how—how will you get there?"

"*Ha!*" the Hag grunted explosively. "Then you didn't know everything, did you? We've planned this for a long time—a colony on Ganymede. We've prepared everything—bred specialized slaves in our laboratories, even built a ship. Oh, you never knew what went on in the Hag Palace!

"The ship alone was an immense project. But you never knew. Listen to me—I'll tell you about it. It's in this very building! The six topmost stories are false—and inside them, all ready for the trip, is a rocket capable of taking us anywhere in the System!"

She stepped back, mock sympathy on her face. She turned to the wall, swung out a panel and carefully turned a knob concealed behind it.

"That gives you eight more minutes of life," she announced. "In five minutes the ship takes off—and, three minutes after that, the timer will set off enough U-Two-thirty-five to blast this building to powder!"

She waved a sardonic farewell and walked past them, out into the corridor without a backward glance. In a moment they heard the closing of an elevator door—then silence.

"Try to get loose!" Valentine ordered as soon as the Hag was out of earshot. "Squirm—twist around—it's our only chance." He was straining every muscle himself but it was useless. Against the steel tentacles of the robot his strength was impotent.

"Can't do a thing," Hanley panted. "Listen, if all the Hags are leaving for the ship what makes this thing keep on holding us?"

"That's what it's set to do—it'll keep on holding us until the controls at the other end of the cable are set for something else. Or until we all blow up." Valentine abruptly stopped squirming.

It did no good. The only thing that could help him then was thought. Brow furrowed, he stared at the floor, his mind racing. He gazed absently at the snakelike black cable . . .

"That's it!" he whooped. "Hanley—can you reach that cable with your feet? You're nearest."

Hanley strained. "Yeah," he reported. "What do I do?"

"Try to pull it out of its socket! They can't have had time to do a good job. Kick it loose!"

Hanley, stretching his leg to the limit, managed to slip a toe under the curling length of the cable. He kicked—but the cable slipped away before he could accomplish his purpose. He swore, tried again. This time it happened! There was a sharp electrical hiss and a puff of acrid blue smoke. The robot's tentacles tightened on them convulsively, bruising their already tortured bodies. Then they slacked and fell away.

"I got a shock," Hanley complained, rubbing his foot.

"Never mind that!" Valentine darted over to the panel in the wall, stared desperately at the knob the Hag had turned. That was all there was, just the knob with a pointer on a dial graduated in minutes, nothing else. After a quick inspection Valentine grasped the knob and tried to turn it. It would not turn, no matter how much he forced it.

"No use," he said dismally. "It only turns one way, apparently—and I'm afraid to try to shut it off altogether. We'll have to make a run for it." He turned to the sleeping Elena Orris, slapped her ruthlessly. She didn't respond. "We'll have to carry her."

"I'll take her," Hanley offered. "Come on, let's get

out of here." He picked up the girl and hurried out of the door, down toward the stairs. Darl started to follow, then turned to look at Valentine.

"Go ahead," he ordered, his face wrinkled with thought. "I'll be with you in a second."

They made it down the long flights of stairs in record time. On the lowest level of the Palace they encountered the vanguard of the Earthies, milling around in indecision under the inadequate leadership of Ensign Drake. But they responded to Valentine's shouted warnings and every human was out of danger when it happened.

Hanley was just gasping, "It's about time for that ship of theirs to be blasting off," when there was a mighty thunder of sound and the entire Hag Palace seemed to bulge and crumble. The concussion sent them flying into each other, sheltered though they were from the direct blast.

Debris rained for blocks around but they had been warned, and were hugging the walls of the buildings. There were a few casualties among the Earthies—men hurt by flying stone—but no one was killed. And the Hags were destroyed.

"What happened?" Hanley asked in awe. "Why didn't their ship get away?"

"It didn't have a chance," Valentine said soberly. "The timer for the U-Two-thirty-five only worked in one direction. I couldn't stop it or set it back to give us more time. But I could set it ahead. I set it three and a half minutes faster—and it went off right on schedule, thirty seconds before their blast-off time."

Hanley nodded, looking around. An Earth surgeon was bending over Elena Orris with the Space-Fleet ensign hovering anxiously in the background. As he watched she stirred and looked up, jerking her head away from the stimulant capsule the surgeon had crushed under her nose.

Hanley looked at Valentine and Darl, standing behind him in the sheltering doorway of a residence

building. Valentine's arm was around the girl, and
Hanley regarded them with pleasure. Then, surprised,
he saw her face suddenly cloud.

She jerked away.

"Valentine!" she said. "Valentine, you—you heel!"

Startled, Valentine looked down at her. Darl's eyes
were flashing in abrupt anger.

"I'm a little bit slow in understanding things," she
said tautly. "Forgive me. I've been so rushed, I haven't
had time to think."

"What are you talking about?" Valentine asked
bewilderedly.

"You know what I'm talking about! Your deception!"

"What deception?"

"What you said to me in the car! Telling me that you
loved me—kissing me—just so you could get me to close
my eyes, so that the Hags wouldn't be able to see where
we were going. It was all a trick—and I fell for it!"

Valentine looked at her for a searching moment.
Then, without turning his head, he said, "Hanley, go
visit somebody else for a while. As a personal favor."

Grinning, Hanley turned on his heel and strolled
toward the Earthies. But as he walked away he heard
Valentine saying softly, "Darl—that was part of it. I admit it. I couldn't just ask you to close your eyes—it
would have made the Hags suspicious. The easiest way
to do it was to make love to you. Don't you understand?
It was the only way I could do it."

"Yes . . . yes, I suppose so," Darl said, almost sob-
bing. "It's just that I made such a fool of myself, with
all those horrid old harpies watching. And that was all it
meant to you—just a trick."

Valentine shook his head. "No, that wasn't all," he
said gently. He stepped closer to her, holding out his
arms. He whispered, "Darl, there's nobody watching
now."